Patricia Yager Delagrange

passing through brandiss

ALAMEDA, CALIFORNIA

Digital ISBN: 9781954395077
Print ISBN: 9781954395060

To my daughter Allessandra.
Without you, this book would never have been written.
I love you "sempiternal".

CHAPTER ONE

"Hey, those are for Rafe." The guilty look on Cameron's face made Annie laugh.

Cameron's hand hovered a moment over the plate of chocolate chip cookies before he snatched one. "For the road. Rafe's got plenty left."

Annie looked up from the box she asked Cameron to haul down from the attic earlier that day. "Where are you off to now?" She blew out a puff of air to move her bangs out of her eyes.

"I promised to mend Eugenia's mailbox and since she bribed us with cookies, it better be today. Don't want her taking them back."

"You're off to Home Depot?" Annie stood, leaned back and looked up at the ceiling. "Oh, I need a back rub."

Cam wiggled his eyebrows up and down. "How about tonight?" He wrapped his arms around her waist and pulled her toward him. "Is there anything you want me to pick up for you? Mascara? Lipstick? Conditioner?"

"You're such a smart ass." She planted a kiss on the dimple just to the side of his mouth. "I think I'm fine in the beauty department, thanks. Will you be back in time for lunch?"

"No problem. I should find Rafe. See if he wants to go with me."

Their son was all boy, and never passed up an opportunity to tag along with his dad, especially to the hardware store. Annie shook her head. "Sorry, not this time. He's over at Spencer's house, and they're in the middle of a school project. It's due Monday."

Cam shrugged and pulled Annie tighter against his chest. "A kiss for the road?" He pulled off the scrunchy holding her hair in a ponytail.

She stared into his deep brown eyes. "Just one kiss for now. But hey, there could be more in the future. If you're lucky."

"I look forward to it." He kissed her full on the mouth. "Right after *America's Most Wanted*."

He turned and she slapped him on the butt before he ran out the side door leading to the garage and jumped in his truck.

Through the kitchen window Annie watched him back out of the driveway and blew a kiss in his direction. He waved and tooted the horn.

* * * *

Rafe needed pictures of his parents, as well as the three of them together, for his project titled "My Family," to complete the assignment. Annie lost track of time, her mind buried deep in memories as she turned the pages of the photo album lying on the kitchen table.

She glanced up at the clock. Almost two hours had flown by and Cam should have returned by now. She grabbed the mayonnaise and turkey out of the fridge to make sandwiches.

The phone's cutesy ringtone began its irritating song. Annie allowed Rafe to pick his favorite and he insisted it was the best of the bunch. With a promise to herself that she'd change it later, she picked up the cordless handset.

"Mrs. Davidson, please." The voice on the other end of the line was both male and authoritative. Annie hated when telemarketing companies called on the weekend.

"This is Annie Davidson."

"This is Sergeant Velez of the Mill Valley Police Department. I'm sorry, Mrs. Davidson, but your husband has been in an accident. He's being transported by ambulance to the University of California San Francisco Hospital. I think it would be a good idea if you got there as soon as possible."

Annie pressed the phone against her ear so hard it hurt. Oddly enough, the first thought that came to her mind was one of Cam's buddies at the job site was playing a bad practical joke on her. When she didn't hear any laughing on the other end of the line, it quickly sank in.

This was not a prank call.

"What happened? Is Cameron alright? Was he injured?" She blurted questions like automatic gunfire, afraid of the answers.

"Mrs. Davidson, your husband's truck was broadsided by an eighteen-wheeler at around twelve-thirty p.m. It was a serious accident, ma'am. Is someone available to take you to the hospital?"

The words stopped making sense, suddenly distant, beyond hearing. Annie tried to focus.

"Do you know where U.C.S.F. is, Mrs. Davidson?"

"Uh, yes... I do. I'm leaving right away." She placed the phone back in its cradle and stared out the kitchen window at the front lawn, green and lush. The mail carrier stuffed a wad of envelopes into the mailbox near the sidewalk.

She had to leave. Cameron was on his way to U.C. San Francisco. But why hadn't they taken him to Marin General, practically around the corner from their house? Were his injuries extensive enough to warrant the significantly longer drive to the much larger Trauma Center?

She snagged her purse off the table and raced to the car. "Oh, my God. Rafe." He told Annie he'd be home by five o'clock. It was almost two p.m. now, and she had no idea how long she'd be at the hospital.

She reached for her cell phone to call Eugenia, their next-door neighbor, and arranged for her to sit with Rafe until she returned.

She could not break down, not when she didn't know how bad things were yet. Her tears held in check, she drove as fast as she could over the Golden Gate Bridge, anxious to get to the hospital as soon as possible. She swerved the Mercedes in and out between clogged lanes of Saturday traffic.

In less than twenty minutes, Annie pulled into the underground parking lot at the hospital, raced into the building and reached the elevator just as the doors were closing. People crowded the reception area on the ground floor and only three receptionists were working at the front desk.

She twisted a long strand of hair round and round her finger and waited her turn in line. The young girl put her index finger in the air and answered another call before she glanced up at Annie.

"Cameron Davidson," Annie said in a shaky voice. "Is he still in the E.R.?"

The receptionist scanned the computer, picked up the phone and made a call. "He's still in the Emergency Room, but they should be moving him to the ICU soon. Are you a member of the family?"

"I'm his wife."

"The ICU is on the fourth floor. There's a designated waiting room to the left when you exit the elevator." She pointed to the bank of elevators behind her.

Annie thanked her, rushed around the counter and angled herself to fit into the one elevator that remained open. Her legs twitched while she waited to reach the fourth floor. With an annoying "ping," the doors slid open, and Annie stepped into the unknown.

CHAPTER TWO

Though scattered with nurses and interspersed with men and women in blue scrubs, an eerie silence reigned within the central hub of the ICU. Everyone spoke in soft tones, pointed at computer screens before rushing off to patient rooms in slip-resistant shoes.

Annie jogged to the chest-high counter and didn't wait to be noticed. "Excuse me?" Her voice came out in a half-whisper and she cleared her throat. "Nurse?"

A gray-haired woman turned in her direction. Both hands scurried across a computer keyboard, phone propped up against her shoulder. "May I help you?"

"My name's Annie Davidson. My husband's in the E.R. I was told they'll be sending him here to the ICU."

The woman finished her call and walked over to the counter. "Cameron Davidson?" Annie nodded. "He's been taken to X-ray. Why don't you wait in the room around the corner? I'll send Dr. Tsao to see you as soon as she arrives."

Annie thanked her and walked in the direction she indicated. The sign on the wall read 'Visitors for ICU Patients Only', and she entered the small oblong-shaped room. Tacky naugahyde chairs lined one side of the room. A lamp stood on a small table in the far corner.

She sat down, pressed her hands on top of her shaking legs and looked around. Out-of-date magazines covered the table—Field & Stream, Vogue, Good Housekeeping. She picked up a tattered Vogue and thumbed through several pages, unable to think of anything but what Dr. Tsao would tell her when she arrived.

Annie closed her eyes and took three deep cleansing breaths, staring at the lilies in the print on the wall. Her zinging nerves refused to calm down. Each time she flipped open her cell phone, only two or three minutes had gone by.

At ten p.m., a young Asian woman with a stethoscope hanging around her neck rounded the corner. "Mrs. Davidson?"

Annie jumped up and extended her hand. "I'm Cameron Davidson's wife. Dr. Tsao?"

Dr. Tsao shook Annie's hand. "Your husband's been moved to Room 405 in the ICU. We took a complete CAT scan, head to toe." With a nod, the doctor indicated the nearest chair then took a seat next to Annie, angling her body in Annie's direction.

Annie crossed her arms over her chest, squeezing herself in a tight embrace. "He's going to make it, right?"

Dr. Tsao covered Annie's hand lightly with her fingers. "Your husband sustained a TBI, traumatic brain injury. He's suffering from cerebral edema. Swelling inside of the brain. Under other circumstances, we'd operate, but unfortunately, his liver, spleen, and kidneys are bleeding."

Pins and needles poked at Annie's legs and she stood up, glancing down at the magazines. On the cover of Field and Stream a man dressed in waders held up a huge fish. Its glassy button of an eye stared up at Annie's face. She chewed her bottom lip and looked at Dr. Tsao. "Could he be placed on the organ transplant waiting list?"

Dr. Tsao stood up and held Annie's gaze. The abyss widened between them. The chasm created by the doctor's medical knowledge and Annie's ignorance of what could keep Cameron from dying enlarged with every passing moment.

"He's not stable enough to undergo surgery, Mrs. Davidson. Machines are keeping him alive. He's in a deep coma."

Annie slumped down into the chair and shook her head, refusing to believe Cam wouldn't pull through this, that he and Annie wouldn't get their happily ever after like in the movies.

Dr. Tsao reached out and touched Annie's shoulder. "Go see him, Mrs. Davidson."

Annie knew damn well what the doctor was trying to tell her and followed her past the nurse's station. Dr. Tsao stopped in front of Room 405 and patted Annie lightly on the back and continued down the hall.

Mauve drapes covered the glass walls of Room 405, the numbers stenciled in black across the glass. Annie took one deep breath before crossing through mental quicksand into Cameron's room.

A cream-colored blanket covered him from the waist down, a white sheet folded over at the edge. Gauze shielded the top part of his head and a black accordion tube snaked out of his mouth. Machines surrounded his bed, blinking and beeping, the rhythm oddly calming.

He was alive.

Annie laced her fingers with his and squeezed, willing her energy to pass through him, as if her touch could keep him more alive than the contraptions. She leaned over the side of the bed, kissed his cheek, inhaling the sickeningly sweet scent of Betadine.

Suddenly the beeps burst to life, louder, more insistent and irritating. A thin blue line, straight and flat, slid across the black screen on the monitor above his bed.

Firm hands grasped Annie's shoulders and pulled her away from his bedside.

"What are you doing? Stop! What's happening?"

A nurse tugged on Annie's arm and led her through the doorway. "Mrs. Davidson. You have to leave the room. Now."

Annie glanced back at Cam before passing the room's threshold, shuffled backward into the hallway and banged against the wall. Doctors and nurses raced from all directions and funneled to Cam's bedside.

She stared at the closed door to Cameron's room, her eyes burning. "Please, God, save him. I need him. Rafe needs him. Don't let him die." No matter how busy God was, helping other people in the world, perhaps Annie's personal plea would reach Him.

She envisioned a happy scenario. Cam was going to pull through. She knew it.

The door swung open. Dr. Tsao walked out slowly, eyes and head angled down until she reached the middle of the wide hallway. Annie pushed away from the wall. Their eyes met.

The doctor didn't have to say a word. The downward twist of her lips, the flat glaze of her eyes. Annie knew Dr. Tsao wouldn't be uttering the words she hoped to hear.

"I'm sorry, Mrs. Davi-"

Annie turned and rushed to the end of the hallway toward the brightly lit exit sign, pushed the lever on the door, and ran down five flights of concrete stairs to the parking garage. She found the car, unlocked the door, and drove out of the garage, heading across the Golden Gate Bridge toward Sausalito.

The first exit at the end of the bridge led to the GGNRA, the local acronym for the Golden Gate National Recreation Area—thousands of acres of state-owned land covered in rolling hills and unused military barracks.

She took the exit and stopped the car on the side of the road. Silence rang in her ears. Silhouettes of horses drifted across the darkened pasture. Crickets chirped. An owl hooted. Alone now, Annie's wails of misery cut through the night, high-pitched howls echoing off the hillsides.

Time stood still. Stuck in that final second when she'd seen Cam alive, when she turned her head to take her last look at him.

It was over.

He was over.

They were over.

It was only Rafe and Annie now.

And Annie couldn't remember ever feeling so utterly and indescribably alone.

CHAPTER THREE

Annie pulled into the garage and sat in the car as the cooling engine ticked and time pulsed by. Seconds or minutes, perhaps an hour, passed before she walked into the kitchen. The rich aroma of Columbian coffee wafted through the silence of her home. Eugenia met her in the kitchen doorway and pulled Annie toward her ample waistline. Eugenia patted Annie's back and murmured indecipherable words of comfort. Annie let Eugenia lead her toward the kitchen table where she pulled out a chair.

Eugenia grasped Annie's shoulder, guided her into the seat, poured coffee into a mug and placed it on the table. Eugenia's footsteps faded away, the front door latch clicked, and Annie knew her friend had returned to her house next door.

* * * *

The sun's glow nudged the night sky. Brushstrokes of yellow streaked across the horizon. Sunrise in Sausalito. The day was beginning for the rest of the world, but Annie's entire world had come to an end.

Cameron was never coming home.

Rafe entered the kitchen and kissed Annie on the cheek. She turned toward him and wrapped her arms around his slender frame. Her tears flowed onto the shoulder of her son's pajamas.

He pulled out of her embrace with a puzzled expression. "Where's Daddy?"

How was she going to do this? How could she say the words that she knew would change Rafe's world forever?

"He made me promise to tell you he loves you very much, more than anyone on this earth, Rafe." Had Cameron been lucid, he would have said those exact words.

"He's not coming home," he whispered.

Annie couldn't sugar-coat the crushing truth. "No, he's not, Honey."

He slumped toward the floor. Annie pulled him onto her lap and held him while he sobbed. There wasn't a damn thing she could say to her nine-year-old-son that would bring his father back.

Several minutes passed before Rafe wrenched out of his mother's arms, tore across the room and slammed his bedroom door. Rafe's quiet little world had been shattered for the first time ever. And Annie had no clue how either of them would deal with this.

Rafe didn't want to come out of his room, and the funeral was in three days. Annie enticed him with doughnuts and hot cocoa for breakfast, but Rafe wouldn't talk. He refused to answer her questions about how he was feeling or engage in conversation about Cam's death.

She brought him lunch in his bedroom, but he wouldn't eat, claiming he wasn't hungry, hunched over his Nintendo DS playing video games. Each night, Annie fixed his favorite meals, and they ate together in silence. He'd pick at a small portion of the food on his plate before he'd escape back into his bedroom.

He'd shut down, and Annie could only hope that, with time, he would find his happy place once again.

* * * *

The black dress she'd worn at both her parents' funerals still hung in the far corner of her closet. All the bad memories returned after she slipped it on. Now she had someone else she loved to add to her repertoire of dead family members.

The ride in the limousine, the memorial service, the burial—Annie experienced them as if they were happening to someone else—her mind's way of sheltering her from the overwhelming sadness.

Rafe stuck to her side like Velcro, a shadow of her own grief, and though most people spoke to him and tried to hug him, he refused to respond.

After the funeral, he spent the rest of the day huddled under the covers in his bedroom. Several of his friends came over with their parents, but he refused to join them.

Everyone was so sorry. They loved Cameron. Such a great guy. On and on. When Annie shut the door behind the last person to leave the reception, she felt exhausted beyond caring. She just wanted to climb into bed and sleep forever.

What the hell was she going to do tomorrow, when life returned to normal? Cam's death was so painfully fresh, yet Rafe would have to go back to school and Annie's personal life would resume. Life hadn't stopped for anyone except the two of them and, by society's standards, they needed to get back to their daily routines.

The following day she approached Rafe. "Honey, you can go back to school on Monday if you feel up to it."

He lifted his gaze to meet hers and her heart twisted. He resembled his father so much.

"Can you drive me?"

Annie tried a full smile, though it felt more like a grimace. "Of course I'll drive you." She patted the seat of the chair beside her, and Rafe sat down.

His eyebrows drew down in a vee. "Daddy always drove me to school."

He was breaking Annie's heart. And he had no clue. She cupped the side of his face in her palm and tried to keep the incessant tears at bay. "We're both sad about Daddy dying, Honey. But we can't sit home and cry all day. We have to learn to live our life without him. That's what he would want us to do. Maybe being with your friends at school will make you feel better, help you forget about it for a while."

He stood abruptly and glared at her. "I don't want to forget him." He ran toward his room. "I'll never forget him."

This time he didn't slam his bedroom door, perhaps subconsciously beckoning her to follow. Annie entered his room and sat on the edge of his bed where he laid face down, head buried in the pillow.

"Honey," she whispered.

He sat up and put his arms around Annie's neck.

Her heart swayed, and tears spilled down her cheeks. "I'll make your favorite bologna sandwich with a Hostess cupcake and a box drink for your school lunch. And maybe you can have Spencer over this weekend for a sleepover."

He nodded, pulled away, and smothered his face in the pillow again. Annie weaved her hand through the silky hair on the back of his head and kissed his cheek. She stood and closed the door softly on her way out.

She felt more alone than ever.

And she had to learn how to be a single mom.

Six days after they'd buried the love of her life, Rafe returned to Breakwater Elementary. Annie did the wash, went to the grocery store, performed all the simple tasks that made up a typical day.

But somehow returning to normal made it seem as if Cameron's life hadn't mattered, bordering on the sacrilegious, dishonoring the dead. But what could she do?

She felt adrift, with no one to turn to. Her closest friend, besides her husband, had been her mom, and she was dead as well. Annie always had Cam to lean on.

But that was before.

Three weeks later she sat in her car in front of Rafe's school, waiting to pick him up. Ten minutes passed. All the other children had already left. Rafe was never late.

Annie ran to his classroom and inched her head around the corner. His teacher, Tracy Allegrotti, sat at her desk at the front of the room, Rafe in front of her in the first row with his head down, pencil in hand.

Ms. Allegrotti nodded and walked over to put her hand on Annie's forearm. "Let's talk, Annie."

They walked down the hallway. The sound of their shoes echoed through the silence.

"I tried to call your cell phone, but you didn't pick up," Tracy said.

Annie buried her hand in her purse and searched for her phone. "I don't know where I put it. Is there something wrong?"

"Please, sit." Tracy pointed to a long bench along the side of the hallway. "It's been several weeks since your husband died. Rafe hasn't turned in any homework and he's failed all his tests." She paused.

Annie was sure Tracy could see the expression on her face because Tracy covered her hand gently and squeezed.

"Annie, I didn't notify you before this because I wanted to give Rafe some time to process his father's death."

Annie leaned back against the wall and closed her eyes for a second. "I always helped him with his reading homework and Cam helped him with math. But for the last three weeks, he's been telling me he's okay, that he doesn't need my help. He's in his room for a couple of hours, comes out, eats dinner, goes back in his room. I assumed he was doing his school work.

"I'm trying not to smother him, Tracy. I wanted to give him his space to think and process Cam's death." She leaned forward, cradled her head in her hands. "What should I do? He refuses to talk about it."

Tracy slipped a business card into Annie's hands. "Caitlin is a great family therapist."

Annie glanced at the card and nodded.

"You might both want to see her, Annie."

Annie thanked her, and they walked back to the classroom. Rafe faced the window, an empty sheet of paper on his desk.

"Let's go, Honey," Annie said.

He stuffed books and papers into his backpack, and they walked down the hall and out the front doors.

After Annie pulled out of the parking lot, she glanced at him. He chewed on his fingernails—a new habit since Cam's death.

"I'll be helping you with your homework from now on, just to make sure you understand what's going on in class. And I'll quiz you right before the tests."

Silence.

"Would you like to invite Spencer over one of these nights and I'll order a pizza?"

"No, thanks."

"Honey, Ms. Allegrotti gave me the name of a nice woman who we could talk to. It might help both of us accept your father's death and move on."

"I don't want him to be gone."

Annie pulled into the garage and turned off the car. Rafe bolted through the door connected to the kitchen before she'd pulled the key from the ignition.

This was going to be hard.

He'd shut his bedroom door. She knocked softly and turned the knob. He lay face down on his bed.

"Honey, can we talk?"

"I don't wanna talk. And I'm not going to some counselor. You can't make me."

She rubbed his back and he turned his head toward her. "I don't want to make you do anything, Rafe. But Ms. Allegrotti told me you aren't doing your homework and you're not passing the tests. You don't want to have your friends over. I know you're sad about your dad and sometimes talking about it helps you get through the bad times. I don't have to be in the room with you and the counselor, if you don't want me to."

He turned onto his back and stared at the ceiling. "I don't even know her. Why would I talk to her about anything?"

"Because she's a psychologist. That means her job is to help people who are sad and unhappy about stuff. If you talk to her, you might feel better. It's worth a try. It can't hurt you."

He hesitated. Annie could almost see the wheels turn inside his head while he contemplated her suggestion.

"You'll come with me?"

"I could wait outside or come in with you—whichever you want. I'm going to talk to her, too, Rafe, to see if she can help me. I'm having a hard time since your daddy died, too."

He turned his head toward her, his forehead furrowed. "Really?"

Annie grasped his forearm and nodded. "Of course, Honey. I loved your daddy so much. And everywhere I turn I see him and it's so hard for me. I lie in bed at night missing him. I wake up missing him. Being in this house reminds me that he's not here any longer."

His head moved up and down oh-so-slowly while she was talking and she knew she'd hit a chord.

He turned onto his side and shut his eyes. "Okay."

Annie breathed a sigh of relief and kissed his forehead.

She hoped Caitlin would turn out to be their salvation.

CHAPTER FOUR

A cold wind whipped across the cemetery grounds, swirling long tendrils of hair across Annie's face, obscuring her view of the casket. Leaves wended their way through the gravestones and covered the top of the coffin in an artistic collage of orange and brown.

The force of the breeze shook her off balance and her foot slipped downward in the wet dirt. She pitched forward, arms shooting out to break her fall. Her head and upper body hit the wood first and her legs and feet draped over the sides, her chest embedded in the raised wood of the coffin's surface.

Pieces of wet earth filled her nostrils. Damp leaves clung to her cheeks and forehead. She tried to push upward but her limbs wouldn't budge. She struggled to open her eyes. Her right arm tingled with pinpricks, numb. She wrenched her hand out from under her side and hit it against a hard surface. She rubbed her palm over what felt like the dashboard of her car.

Her eyes fluttered open. Another nightmare, exhausting in its relentless reappearance. Lights flickered in the dark, humming on the poles that rimmed the parking lot. Her body splayed across the front seat of the Mercedes. She felt disoriented, but knew where she was parked—in front of a row of picnic tables at the rest stop.

Falling asleep at the wheel wasn't the way she imagined leaving this world to join Cameron. And she had to think of Rafe, asleep in the back seat. He counted on her to keep him safe. A short nap was all she needed after driving five hours, exhausted from staring at the monotonous freeway lines since leaving the Golden Gate Bridge in their wake.

Recharged, Annie started the car, and exited the rest stop, headed south with no particular destination in mind. Their journey down 101 took them away from Sausalito. That was the only thing that mattered.

Rafe stirred in the back seat and she glanced in the rearview mirror. He sat up and rubbed his eyes with the heels of his hands. "I'm hungry, Mom." He leaned forward and wrapped his arms around her neck.

Annie reached back and mussed his soft hair between her fingers, grabbed the small ice chest on the floor and placed it on the passenger seat. "I've got some of your favorite snacks—cheese, box drinks, orange juice, Hershey bars."

"We're still driving?" He snagged a candy bar and ripped off the wrapper.

Annie glanced back at him for a second. "Honey, we talked about this before we left."

"I know." He sat back, leaned his head against the headrest and shut his eyes.

"Rafe?"

"Yeah?"

"I don't think you forgot."

"No." In a sing-song voice, he said, "Let's see where the road leads us and if we don't like where we are, we can always move back." He groaned. "Are we gonna stop somewhere to eat soon?"

He was almost eleven-years-old, his stomach a bottomless pit. "We'll stop to get a bite to eat soon. Can you wait?" Annie's gaze met his in the rearview mirror and he grinned.

"I can do that," he said.

"Yeah, Rafe, you can do that."

Freeway driving had never been one of Annie's favorite ways to spend her time either, but she loved the drive along PCH - Californians' endearing title for the Pacific Coast Highway which runs parallel along the jagged coastline of California. The western edge of the map reminded her of the blips on an EKG.

She gave her head a quick shake. The incessant replay of the night Cam died was mentally exhausting. Her mind kept pushing the rewind button to that evening in the ICU.

"Look!" Rafe pointed toward the passenger side window.

Heaving waves broke along the sandy shore. "Looks like a picture," she said. "Remember when we had a bonfire on the beach when you were seven years old? We roasted a whole bag of marshmallows."

"And I almost barfed because I ate too many."

Annie smiled to herself. "We had fun, didn't we? We watched the sun go down and wrapped up in blankets around the fire."

The Pacific Ocean, simply another on her list of experiences that she and Cam would never share. Oh, the constant reminders, the sole reason they'd left their home, to escape to a new place so the memories of Cameron could finally, one day, bring a smile to her lips, a soft tear to her cheek.

After a year and a half of counseling sessions with Caitlin, Annie assumed she'd feel normal again. But as the months went by, she still didn't feel like her old self. Her mind was living in the same body, but her mental state was not what it once had been.

Caitlin had helped both of them accept that Cam was dead, that he was never coming back, that they could hold the memories in their hearts of all the days they'd spent with him and smile at the wonderful scrapbook of their lives together before the accident.

But as the months dragged on, every time she went to bed at night and saw the empty pillow on the opposite side of bed, her heart squeezed and the tears still flowed. Cam was everywhere.

And by the pinched expression around Rafe's eyes each time they drove by the many houses Cam and his crew had built in Sausalito, she could tell that he was trying not to cry. Cam was everywhere for him, too.

Living in their home in Sausalito had become a daily reminder that Cam was no longer a part of their world. Cam's favorite chair, his tools, the cup he always used for coffee. It was as if Rafe and Annie were waiting for Cam to suddenly show up one day and they'd continue on, as if nothing had ever happened.

And when Rafe and Annie went to the park, or the hardware store, or the movie theatre, they were reminded of what Cam had said or done or laughed about when he was there with them.

Finally, Rafe and Annie agreed to leave their home in Sausalito and try something new.

"Do you see over there, on the other side of the freeway?" Rafe said.

The cherry blossom trees were beginning to show their tiny pink flower buds, Annie's personal favorites. The same trees that appeared in the movie *The Last Samurai*. Whenever they burst into bloom,

Annie always made Cam stop the car so she could take a longer look.

Annie laughed under her breath. "You mean the cows on the hills, munching on the grass?"

"You know what I'm talking about, Mom. The cherry trees."

"Why don't we take the next turn-off and stretch our legs?"

The next exit sign read "Route A33/Brandiss". She'd driven the 101 many times on her way to visit her sister Kathy in Lakeside, east of San Diego, but she didn't remember ever seeing this exit.

She slowed the car to a crawl, grabbed the map and scanned the details of this area. Nothing indicated a Route A33 or a place called Brandiss. Maybe the map was outdated. It had been in the glove compartment for years, with the requisite folds and smudges from numerous handlings.

Annie took the turnoff anyway and came to a halt at the stop sign at the bottom of the grade. A sign pointed left to Route A33/Brandiss. She pulled out and headed toward the rolling hills, cows, and beautiful weeping cherry trees.

CHAPTER FIVE

Route A33 reminded Annie of the last scene from the movie *The Bridges of Madison County*. The road slowly meandered up then glided down, like a gentle roller coaster. No houses were visible from the car, no side roads, no other cars on the road, nothing but cherry trees and cows.

She drove over another rise, reached the crest, and there, on the right side of the road, was a sign that read: Brandiss, Estab. 1919. Underneath was written: Population: 1,395.

"Wow! All the years I've driven to Southern California, I've never heard of Brandiss. This is like discovering a lost city, Rafe."

Rafe studied the map, his finger moving along the lines and dots. "I don't see it here, either." His nose almost touched the crinkled paper.

Annie slowed to fifteen miles per hour. They could have walked faster than she was driving. The sign indicated she was driving down Main Street. Side streets ran off to the left and right with names such as Peach Way and Apple Court.

"Hey, Rafe, keep an eye out for a place for us to eat lunch, okay? You hungry?"

"I'm starving," he yelled, face plastered against the glass.

The little town of Brandiss appeared so peaceful, located far enough off the beaten track that few people would travel it. Annie didn't know where Route A33 headed. It meandered out of town and no signs indicated cities or towns east of the town.

"I don't know about you, Rafe, but I want to see where this road leads."

"But I can't find Brandiss on the map," he grumbled. "And I don't see one of those squiggly lines for Route A33 either."

She laughed and continued down Main Street. "Well, they exist, Rafe, because we're here, aren't we?"

"What if we get lost?" he said, his voice oh-so-serious. "If the road doesn't lead us anywhere we don't have any more food in the car."

She'd driven only a few blocks down the street when a real estate sign appeared on top of a white sawhorse: Open House, Noon to Five. A big red arrow pointed down the street.

"Look, Rafe. A house for sale."

Rafe peered out the side window of the passenger seat. "At least we won't have to stay in this stupid car any longer," he said, his voice heavily tinged with sarcasm.

Annie rolled her eyes and turned down the cul-de-sac. Rafe disliked long drives but she didn't blame him. She'd felt the same way when she was his age.

"You want to take a look?" Annie said.

He pointed at a yellow sign at the end of the street. "It says 'Dead End,' Mom."

"I just saw it, too, Honey. That just means we have to turn around when we leave. Don't worry." She slowed to get a better look at the houses. The second sawhorse appeared in front of the house for sale and she pulled over and parked.

She pointed at the Craftsman-style home. "Looks like something you'd see on the cover of a book."

He rolled down the passenger side window. "You read so many books, Mom. Which one are you talking about?"

"I just meant... ," Annie began, then sighed. Rafe was relentlessly inquisitive. At times it was exhausting. "I think it was a book written by Debbie Macomber, my favorite author. The book jackets always look so cozy. I just want to crawl inside the picture on the cover and... "

"Read?" He burst out laughing.

She gave him a withering look. "Oh, you're just sooo funny." She grabbed the door handle. "Let's walk through it. I love all the grass in the front yard and the white picket fence. It's got a pergola, too."

His hand clutched the door handle, and he glanced over his shoulder at her. "A pergola?"

"Yeah, like a trellis. See the front gate? Hanging over it is what's called a pergola. Wow, it's totally covered in roses." Annie stepped out of the car and waited for Rafe to get out.

"It might be totally gross inside," he said, too loudly.

She came around to his side of the car and bent down. "If it's gross," she whispered, "we'll walk out and drive away. Okay?"

"Where will we go?"

Annie expelled a huge breath of air and tweaked his nose. "Could we puh-leeze just make it to the front door before you ask me any more questions?"

He grinned and tugged on the edge of her shirt. "Just one more question?"

She leaned down again. "One more question, Rafe," she warned him with a smile.

"If this house is like Melanie's, can we buy it?"

Well aware of his fondness for spacious, turn-of-the-century houses, Annie pressed a quick kiss on the middle of his forehead. "I love old houses too, Rafe. Let's take a look-see. Then we'll talk."

He rushed over to the gate and pulled the string on the latch. They passed under the pergola, dipping their heads through the array of roses that dangled over the wooden slats, the sweet scent permeating the air.

The front door stood open and a folded piece of pink stationary with the words, "Welcome. Come right in" scrolled across the front was propped open on top of a table next to the door.

Annie opened the screen door. "Hello?"

A woman's voice came from somewhere toward the rear of the house. "I'll be right there." An attractive young lady walked toward them, dark brown hair draped along her slender shoulders. "I'm Karen Robins. Feel free to look through the house. I'll be back in the kitchen if you have any questions." She handed Annie a piece of paper with the details concerning the property.

"Has the house been on the market long?" Annie asked and glanced down at the detailed information.

"It's been for sale for a few months. It was built in 1908 and the original owner, Barbara Ivy, passed away earlier this year. Her relatives put it up for sale. I guess no one wanted to come all the way from Ohio to live in California." She paused. "Go figure, right?"

Annie chuckled. "I'm a born and bred California girl myself." She stretched out her hand. "I'm Annie Davidson and this is my son, Rafe."

Karen shook Annie's hand firmly, turned, and took hold of Rafe's outstretched hand. "Nice to meet you both. California's such a beautiful state. And the weather just can't be beat."

"You're right about that," Annie said. "Well, thank you for the information. We'll take a walk-through and talk with you afterward."

Annie and Rafe ambled toward the back of the house. It was so quiet in Brandiss. Mid-week was not exactly a bustling day for selling houses in this off-the-beaten-track little town.

They walked through a large front room with twelve-foot-high ceilings, glowing hardwood floors, and windows that overlooked the front yard and neighboring homes. Rafe pushed aside a wide pocket door made of hundreds of small glass panes, affording them a look into the dining room. A chandelier hung in the middle, decorated with tiny tear-drop crystals. Rafe flipped on the light switch, and the dark wood walls gleamed.

Doors at both the left and right sides at the back of the dining room led to the kitchen at the rear of the house. Karen Robins sat at the center island and smiled as they walked through. The kitchen had been renovated with granite countertops, and oak cupboards lined the walls.

Rafe ran past the laundry room out the back door. Annie followed him, and was pleasantly surprised to see a huge yard. An old oak tree grew on the right. Its branches and leaves shaded half of the luscious green lawn.

Toward the back of the yard, Rafe climbed onto one of the low-slung leather seats of a swing set. His legs pumped back and forth, head tilted up toward the blue sky and white scudding clouds, mouth open to the breeze.

"Come on, Rafe," she shouted, gesturing to him. "Let's go upstairs."

He ran over and they walked through a short hallway toward the foyer. They took the stairs on the right that led up to the second floor. The master bedroom was on the left toward the front of the house, its walls covered in double-hung windows with its own bath and a large claw-foot tub.

Rafe headed to the right toward the other two bedrooms that faced the back. There was a huge bathroom in between with a second claw-foot tub. Newly sanded and varnished hardwood floors glistened throughout the house.

Annie and Rafe met in the hallway. Like her son, she'd never favored tract homes. She expected he'd fallen in love with this house as much as she already had.

"Your Grandma and Grandpa and I lived in a single story house in San Leandro when I was growing up. Your Auntie Kathy and I had to share a bedroom. And the backyard was so small, we always played in the front yard or in the street."

He grinned. "This place is huge, Mom. And the bedrooms are way bigger than our home in Sausalito."

"What about the backyard with that swing set?"

"Are we gonna buy it?" he asked, his dark eyebrows lifted high into his bangs.

"Would you like to live here?"

His expression turned serious. "Are we ever gonna go back home?"

"Honey, after a while I'm sure you'd think of this as your home. If we live here, you'd have to give this place a chance. We'd have to find out what school you'd go to and enroll you. You'd make new friends." She paused. "Remember, Caitlin said we have to put the past behind us but that doesn't mean putting the memories behind us."

Annie swept a lock of hair off his forehead. "You and I don't want to ever forget Daddy. And we shouldn't ever forget him. But Caitlin explained to me how I can't live my life backward. I can only live it from today, forward. Didn't she tell you the same thing?"

He nodded.

"Then we have to try, Rafe. Before we left Sausalito you and I talked about giving ourselves another chance to be happy even though your father won't be with us."

"Yeah."

"Can you picture yourself here in this huge old house, playing in that big backyard?"

He moved his head up and down several times. "I can do that."

"I can do that, too." She clapped her hands together. "Let's go downstairs and talk to Ms. Robins."

On their way back to the kitchen, Annie pictured the house decorated with Tiffany lamps, Irish lace curtains, and antique four-poster beds. She'd fallen in love with it, and felt confident Rafe had, too.

Karen Robins sat on a stool in the kitchen, doodling on a clipboard. She glanced up as they entered. "You two like this house, huh?"

Annie grinned. "How could you tell?"

"Would you like to think about it, call me later? Or do you have any questions I could answer?"

Annie glanced at Rafe, who looked almost scared, his eyes wide. "I think Rafe and I would like to live in this house."

Karen's face lit up. "Well, good for you. Congratulations! Do you have a house you're trying to sell before you buy this one?"

Annie shook her head. "Our house in Sausalito is already sold. This would be a cash deal."

Karen's smile widened. "Would you like to set up a meeting at my office?"

"Any time you're available."

Karen pulled out her day planner, ran her finger down the page and laughed. "It just so happens I have the entire week free." She looked at Annie over the top of the planner. "As you can see, Brandiss is a very, very small town. This job doesn't keep me all that busy whether it's a weekday or the weekend. I sell maybe one house every few months. The realty company I work for is based in Santa Barbara. All the paperwork will be e-mailed to them from my office here in Brandiss." She grabbed a pen. "Tomorrow morning at ten o'clock?"

"Perfect. I'll take one of your cards, if I may." Karen handed Annie her business card. "I'll be at your office at ten tomorrow morning, then." Annie wanted to twirl around right in the middle of the kitchen.

They said goodbye and walked to the car.

"I love the swing set, Mom," Rafe said. "And the backyard has all kinds of cool places to hide. And I can ride my bike in the front, right? It's one of those cool-de-sacs."

"Cul-de-sac," Annie interjected.

At times like this, he acted like the old Rafe. That in itself made Annie's heart sway. But he still had his bad days. She'd find him in the back yard, sitting on the ground with one of the boxcars in the Thomas the Tank Engine gang. He'd mimic Cameron's voice as one of the engines, while he played the part of Thomas. She'd listen to him from around the corner. Invariably the words brought tears to her eyes. He missed his father so much.

"Which bedroom do you want, Honey?"

"The one where the branches almost come inside the windows."

"Oh, you mean the willow tree. That tree must have been growing there since the house was built. It's gigantic."

Rafe's smile grew wide. "Is there an attic?"

Annie hugged him against her side. "Yes, there's an attic. It's got to be much bigger than the one in our house in Sausalito. I didn't go up there, though. How 'bout we make that your adventure? It might be somewhere no man has gone before," she said, referring to his love for anything related to Star Trek.

"Tomorrow I'll meet with Ms. Robins to sign some papers, and then see if I can arrange to have all our things sent here from up north. Maybe we can move in early."

CHAPTER SIX

Annie drove two blocks down Main Street to The Little Inn by the Wayside. She noticed it when she drove into Brandiss—a lovely Victorian house with a garden lush with colorful flowers, twinkling clean windows, and a swing adorning the wrap-around porch.

The cutest little old lady sat in a chair next to the front door. She stood, walked over to the railing, and introduced herself.

"I'm Abigail Wayward. Can I help you?" She blinked through her bifocal glasses.

Annie and Rafe walked to the bottom stair. "Yes, ma'am. My son Rafe and I are buying that beautiful old place that's for sale on Ivy Place. We need somewhere to stay until we move in."

Abigail's red-lipsticked mouth broke into a smile and she gazed off into the distance. "The owner, Barbara Ivy, was one of my closest friends. She'd be happy to know young people will be living there now." She paused, took off her glasses and wiped the lenses with one of the folds of her house dress. "I have a vacancy. You'd be wanting one where you could cook, in case you have to stay several days, eh?" Annie nodded. "Come on in. I'll have you sign in and give you a key."

They followed Abigail into the foyer where she grabbed an old brass key along with a tiny information card that she slid across the top of the desk toward Annie.

Annie quickly filled it out, then the three of them walked up the stairs to the suite, a large room painted egg-shell white, with a high domed ceiling, two single beds and a small kitchen off to one side. Expansive windows faced Main Street and waning sunlight bathed the room. A sun chime tinkled in the corner.

"This is lovely." Annie glanced out the window at the quaint shops lining Main Street then turned toward Abigail. "Thank you very much."

"Welcome to Brandiss," Abigail said. "I think you'll enjoy

living here. Oh, and please call me Abby." She smiled at Annie and Rafe and closed the door behind her.

They plopped down on the sofa that faced the front windows. It had been a long day. And they'd accomplished a great deal in the last twenty-four hours since leaving Sausalito. This little town had a calming effect on Annie. She felt relieved to be in Brandiss, grateful to have discovered it. Slowly but surely, everything seemed to be falling into place.

It was turning dusk, the sun setting behind the tall trees. Golden rays shone through the front windows, the colors changing from bright yellow to orange, to pinkish-purple and finally to deep red.

Annie's eyelids felt heavy and her mind wandered. For months she felt as if she was lying on a raft in the middle of the ocean, surrounded by a vastness so cold and dark, it was impossible for her to know where she was. She couldn't find her bearings, her internal compass broken. She'd been living in a private limbo, adrift and alone.

But both Rafe and she had indeed survived Cam's death. They had each other, and they were going to be all right. And for the first time since Cam's death, Annie believed Rafe and she would find happiness again.

She must have fallen asleep. When she opened her eyes, the sun had disappeared. Her stomach growled. She turned her head toward Rafe and smiled. He'd been the center of her world for years and she loved him unconditionally.

Rafe stirred and his eyes fluttered open. "Hi, Mom."

"Hey, guy. Wanna take a walk to the grocery store? Pick up something to eat?"

He nodded, eyes still puffy from his short nap. "Brandiss Supermarket is right down the street."

After splashing some cool water on her face, Annie snatched the room key from the table and they strolled over to the market. She selected enough items to last for a few days, and took a place at the checkout stand.

A young girl worked the register, helping the person ahead of them. She might have been in her early teens, tall and slender with long blonde hair held up in a ponytail with a scrunchy. Her face without make-up was smooth and lightly tanned, with a small upturned nose and full lips dabbed with a smidgeon of pink lipstick.

"For such a small town, it sure is busy here," Annie said when it was their turn.

The young girl looked up from scanning their groceries and smirked. "This is the place to come if you want excitement, all right."

Annie laughed. "Not a lot happening here, huh?"

"Debit or credit?" she asked, and laughed under her breath.

"Debit, please. What's so funny? No high school dances or bands playing around town?"

She glanced at Annie and shook her head. "People always think small towns are so cutesy when they're really just plain boring." She handed Annie the receipt. "Have a good time during your visit."

"Oh, we'll be staying here permanently," Annie chirped. "I just bought a house on Ivy Place."

Rafe, mesmerized by the young cashier, stared at the girl as if she was the next American Idol.

The girl raised her eyebrows into long straight bangs and plastered a smile on her lips that didn't quite meet her eyes. "Congratulations on your new house."

Annie took the slip from her outstretched hand. "I hope to see you again."

The two headed back to the inn and stopped in front of several shop windows. The temperature was still mild, and the evening breeze tickled at their backs as they ambled along the sidewalk. After dinner they tumbled into bed and fell asleep almost instantly.

The following morning Annie met with Karen Robins. Abby had volunteered to take care of Rafe so Karen and Annie had ample time to wade through the mass of detailed paperwork. Annie walked back to The Little Inn by the Wayside with a huge grin on her face. Soon they'd be living in their new home!

Rafe and Annie spent the next few days walking around Brandiss proper, not driving the car anywhere unless absolutely necessary. They walked east down Main Street to Brandiss Park where Rafe played basketball with several young kids. Then they strolled further in that direction and encountered a large building with dark wooden double doors, one side propped open with a brick.

"Rafe, do you know what that is?" Annie asked, pointing to the name carved in wood above the doorway.

Rafe read out loud, "Brandiss Elementary School," and turned in Annie's direction. "Is this where I'll be going to school?"

"Yes, it is. I called and school starts this Monday."

They walked up the stairs and through the front doors. The janitor was buffing the already gleaming linoleum floors and directed them toward the end of the hallway to the administration office, where several staff members sat at their desks.

Annie stepped up to the counter and a short woman in her early fifties with a pencil stuck behind her ear greeted them. "May I help you?" She glanced at Annie then at Rafe, giving him a friendly smile.

"I called earlier," Annie said. "We're from the San Francisco Bay Area and will be living here. I'd like to enroll my son for school." She fumbled in her purse for Rafe's birth certificate and vaccination documents.

"Yes, I was the person you spoke with." She perused the paperwork, pushed her glasses upward, and angled her head in Rafe's direction. "You're just in time, young man. You won't miss a day of school."

Annie filled out the application forms and they retraced their steps to the front of the building and headed toward the inn. She thumbed through the sheaf of papers she received from the registrar. "Your teacher's name is Ms. Forrester. The receptionist told me she's one of the kids' favorites."

He pursed his lips, his facial expression pensive. After a few seconds, he muttered, "I miss my friends."

Annie stuffed the material inside her purse, turned toward Rafe and clutched his hands. "When we move into our new home and the phone's turned on, you could call your pals in Sausalito. But you'll make new friends at Brandiss Elementary, Honey, just like you did when you started at Breakwater."

With a vague smile on his face, he nodded, and walked briskly off toward the inn, pulling Annie along with him.

He'd been ambivalent about leaving the Bay Area. However, after months of discussion and help from Caitlin, he agreed it was a good idea and looked at their departure as an adventure, an opportunity to go to a place they'd never been before.

Toward the end of the week, Annie received a phone call from Karen Robins. Since it was a cash deal from the sale of Davidson Construction and thanks to modern technology, the escrow papers were ready, and the closing would be in a few weeks.

The owners in Ohio approved Annie and Rafe moving in right away. She'd be one of the few people she knew who actually owned their home, free and clear with no monthly mortgage payments. It felt good.

Annie hung up the phone and turned to Rafe. "The house is ours!"

He grabbed her around the waist, a big smile on his face. "When can we move in?"

"The moving company won't be here until the middle of next week but that doesn't matter, does it?"

He shrugged. "We have our sleeping bags in the back of the car."

"We'll rough it for a day or two."

The next day they packed their suitcases, thanked Abby for her hospitality, and drove the few blocks to Ivy Place.

* * * *

On Monday, they walked to Brandiss Elementary School for Rafe's first day of school. Rafe stopped on the sidewalk in front of the school, surrounded by kids shouting and laughing.

His eyes misted over. "I can do this, right, Mom?"

Annie bent down to his level and gazed into his big brown eyes, so like his father's. "You can do this, Honey. Just like you did on your first day at Breakwater. Our moving to Brandiss is exactly like you said—to go where no man has gone before, like Captain Kirk on Star Trek."

He smiled, the tears dissipating a bit. "You and Dad always took me on the first day of school."

She nodded, her eyes filling with unshed tears. But she would not cry, not now, not when they were starting fresh, leaving behind all their sorrow in Sausalito.

"Uh-huh," Annie said. "And I believe he's watching you right now." She tapped on the middle of his chest with her index finger. "He's right here, in your heart." She brought her finger to her lips, kissed the tip, and pressed it to his lips. "And this is a kiss from him, just like I promised him I'd do. He'll always love you, Rafe, now and forever."

His lips quirked up at the edges. "Infinimore."

"You're right," she laughed. "Infinimore."

He put his arms around Annie's neck, hugged her, and pulled away to grab his lunch out of her hands. "I can do this."

Annie nodded, too afraid her voice would give away all the emotion clogging her throat. He turned and ran up the stairs.

Annie glanced at the blue sky, pictured the Starship Enterprise gliding toward planets where no man had gone before.

Yes, Cameron, your son can do this. And I can do this, too.

Annie grinned, turned, and walked home, to their new home on Ivy Place.

CHAPTER SEVEN

Annie walked in the front door and sat on the floor in the front room. She'd have to shop for furniture to decorate their new "old" house. They'd had a gigantic garage sale before they left Sausalito. Everything had been modern anyway and wouldn't have been appropriate in a house like this one, built in 1908.

Next on her list: planting a vegetable garden. That would necessitate a lot of digging and raking and, without any help, it would take Annie a gazillion years, as Rafe would say. She saw a bulletin board plastered with business cards and want-ads in front of the Brandiss Supermarket and took a walk to peruse the help wanted postings.

While there she picked up a few grocery items then took her place in line. She noticed the same young girl at the cash register who'd helped her the first time Rafe and she shopped there.

The girl scanned the items from Annie's basket and placed the groceries in paper bags. "How are you today?"

"Fine, thank you," Annie said.

The girl's face took on a quizzical expression. "Didn't I see you here a few days ago, with your son?"

Annie chuckled. "That was me."

"You bought Barbara Ivy's place." She took the debit card from Annie's outstretched hand.

"You have quite a memory. In fact, I'm here to check out your bulletin board. I need to hire someone to help me."

She nodded and placed the filled bags back in the cart.

"I want to plant a vegetable garden, maybe some flowers, that type of thing. Do you know anyone who might be interested in earning a little extra cash?"

"My hours are only part-time here 'cause I work after school. I could use the money."

"I just need an extra pair of hands."

"I work here three or four days a week, but the other days I'm free." She grabbed the "Check Stand Closed" sign and placed it on the rubber belt. "I'll help you out with your groceries." She pushed the basket out the door and walked behind Annie as she headed toward her car. "I don't know your name."

"It's Annie. Annie Davidson. And my little boy's name is Rafe."

"I'm Allessandra. People at school call me Allessi, but I prefer Allessandra. That's what my Mom and Dad called me anyway." Her smile disappeared for just a moment.

They reached Annie's car and Allessandra put the bags in the trunk.

"When could you start?"

Allessandra closed the trunk. "Is tomorrow around three-fifteen okay?"

"Perfect. My car will be parked in the driveway. I'm sure you know the place anyway."

"Yeah. Everybody knew Barbara Ivy. She was the oldest living person in Brandiss. Well," she shrugged, "I guess I'll see you tomorrow." She gave Annie a little wave and jogged back toward the market.

Shortly before three o'clock Annie walked to Brandiss Elementary to meet Rafe after his first day of school. He was all smiles and non-stop chatter the entire way home. Annie told him about hiring Allessandra to help with the gardening. After dinner, they played Bingo and Go Fish, then climbed into their sleeping bags for the night.

The next day, promptly at three-fifteen, Allessandra came to the front door, dressed in cut-off jean shorts and a Beyoncé t-shirt.

"You're right on time," Annie said. "I'm impressed." Annie opened the screen door for her. "Would you like some iced tea? I've got some in the cooler since they haven't delivered our refrigerator yet. We'll take it out back while we're gardening."

"Sure. Thanks."

Allessandra followed Annie into the kitchen where Annie poured the tea into two paper cups.

"I don't get this type of hospitality at the market," Alessandra said.

Annie laughed, took her cup, and walked through the laundry

room out the back door. "Watch it. These back steps are steep."

Annie grabbed a rake propped up against the side of the garage and handed Allessandra the shovel. After twenty minutes they were both perspiring. Annie rested her chin on top of the rake and glanced at Allessandra. "Did you grow up in Brandiss?"

Allessandra jammed the shovel into the dirt, rigid determination on her face. "I've lived here my whole life." She turned the shovel over and dumped out the dirt. "I totally dream of leaving this place. You see the same people, over and over, every single day."

"I grew up in the Bay Area. I wanted to get out of there, too, so I went to Europe after college. Do you want to travel?"

Allessandra stared up at the giant oak tree, the look on her face wistful. Or angry? "I wanted to travel, but... It's not gonna happen any time soon." Their eyes met. "I just want to get this over with, and then I'm outta here."

"Get what over with?"

She pointed down at her stomach. "Due on St. Patrick's Day."

"You're pregnant?" Annie whispered.

Allessandra turned over another clump of dirt with the shovel. "Yep. And not lovin' it. But, hey, no one wants to listen to a whining teenager who managed to get herself knocked up on the first try."

Annie put her hand on Allessandra's forearm and gave it a light squeeze. "Don't apologize. I don't think you're whining."

Allessandra wiped the sweat from her forehead with the edge of her t-shirt, looking more lost and sad than pissed off.

"Hey, let's stop for a bit and talk," Annie said. "I don't know anyone in Brandiss, and Rafe and I can only communicate about so much." Annie smiled, trying to lighten the mood that shadowed the young girl's features.

"I don't have any brothers or sisters, and my Mom and Dad are dead."

"I'm sorry. What happened to them?"

She took a shaky breath. "They were flying home in a small plane from a second honeymoon trip. A bunch of geese flew in one of the engines and the plane went down. It took the rescue people over a week to find them."

Annie frowned. "That must have been horrible. When did this happen?"

"Last year. I've been living with my cousin Stacey and my Aunt Barb. Barb has legal custody of me until I turn eighteen 'cause that's how my Mom and Dad set up their will... so I wouldn't have to do the foster home thing. The money I inherited is in the bank, and Aunt Barb uses it for whatever stuff I need. I can move out soon though, when I turn eighteen." She shrugged. "But for now, it's cool."

Annie gestured toward Allessandra's belly. "So you're about three months along?"

"The doctor said I'll be twelve weeks on September third—in a few days actually. The guy moved back to Mexico. He was earning money in the U.S. to help out his family down there."

"Does he know he's the father?"

She shook her head. "Probably won't ever know."

"Will you and the baby live with your aunt and cousin?"

She shook her head again. "I don't think I'm gonna keep it. I'm seventeen years old. I haven't finished high school. I wanna travel around the U.S. My Aunt Barb said I could use the money from my parents if I had the baby, but there isn't that much money. She thinks I should use the money for, like, college... my future."

"And you? What do you want to do?"

"I don't think I can take care of a baby. And Stacey wants to travel with me. Everyone says adoption's the best thing to do. But I don't know how long it takes to get your baby adopted, or how long I'd have to wait to find somebody."

"Well, you have plenty of time to think about it. Don't push yourself into anything you don't feel one-hundred-percent comfortable with."

She nodded. Annie glanced at what they'd accomplished. One section of the rich brown dirt was now free of pebbles and rocks.

"I think we're done for the day," Annie said. "I have to pick up Rafe from school. Then we're going to look for furniture at the antique store on Main Street." They walked around the side of the house toward the front yard. "Will I see you tomorrow?"

"Yep." She jumped on her bicycle and pedaled off down the street.

Annie's heart went out to this young girl with the heavy burden of deciding what to do about the child she was carrying. Annie wished there was some way she could help her make such an adult decision.

CHAPTER EIGHT

The moving truck arrived the following morning. By the time Rafe came home from school, the few pieces of furniture Annie kept were in place and their personal belongings in their rooms. The few pieces she purchased on Main Street would be delivered the following day.

When Rafe noticed his bicycle leaning against the porch railing, he let out a loud whoop, jumped on it, and was off. It was the same bike he'd owned since he was eight-years-old and, though a bit too small for him now, he loved the freedom of tooling up and down the street.

Annie sat in her favorite rocker in her bedroom in front of the window that overlooked the street where she watched Rafe. She recalled her conversation with Allessandra the day before.

Having carried Rafe for nine months, knowing how much she and Cameron had wanted him, she remembered all the months of worry and hope that he'd be healthy. She couldn't imagine giving up her child, knowing the baby would be better off with someone else.

When Allessandra came over later that day, they picked up their gardening tools and began the tedious job of carving precise rows of dirt for the vegetables they'd be planting. Birds chirped in the nearby trees. A light breeze tipped the edges of the oak leaves.

"It's too quiet. I hate it," Allessandra said.

Annie hauled her gaze away from the perfectly straight lane of dirt she was trying to create. "How did you meet the baby's father?"

Allessandra's eyebrows drew down in a vee as if she were deep in thought. "He was part of the crew that was digging the new foundation on our house."

"So your parents knew him?"

"Yeah. But he and I didn't really get together until after they were killed." She shook her head and took hold of the rake, smacked it down hard in the dirt.

"May I ask why you decided not to tell him?"

"Well, for starters, he's Catholic. And his home's in Nogales. He wasn't here legally. He wasn't planning on staying here after he earned enough money to help out his family."

"What does being Catholic have to do with it?"

"He would have to do the right thing and marry me." She paused. "And he wasn't in love with me."

"Do you know that for sure?"

"That he wasn't in love?"

Annie nodded.

"I didn't need to ask him. It was pretty much a one night stand sorta thing." Her face tinged pink and she turned back around.

"So you two weren't boyfriend and girlfriend?"

She sighed.

"I'm sorry. I shouldn't be so nosey. It's none of my business."

Allessandra turned toward Annie again, mouth set in a straight line. "No, no. I don't think you're being nosey. It's just... " She paused and stared over Annie's head into the distance. "He was the first guy I'd ever, you know, had sex with. I didn't think I'd get pregnant. I just wanted to see what it was like. And I wasn't gonna do it the first time with someone from school."

"Teenagers can be really bad at keeping that kind of a secret."

"My dumb luck to be so fertile." She smirked.

"Did you consider abortion?"

She bit at her lower lip. "Not seriously. My parents got married after my mom got pregnant. The pictures somebody took at their wedding show them from the waist up." She smiled. "Mom was beautiful. And Daddy was so handsome." Her eyes met Annie's. "If she had an abortion, I wouldn't even be here."

"Good point."

"What about you? Do you believe in abortion?"

"I'd never have one, but I believe in a woman's right to choose."

"You're obviously not Catholic."

Annie shrugged. "I was baptized a Catholic, went to St. Felicitas Grammar School. I was raised Catholic."

"Me, too. So you know abortion's a sin."

Annie didn't answer right away.

"Annie?"

"You're right, it's a sin."

"Abortion's okay because the world's overpopulated?" Her voice rose higher with each word. "It's all right to kill an unborn kid just 'cause there are too many foster kids waiting to be adopted?"

"I didn't say that, Allessandra."

"I even think puppy mills should be abolished because too many dogs are being euthanized every day. And people aren't dogs. Abortion's way worse."

"I know."

She looked as if she was about to cry. "Then how can you believe in abortion?"

Annie drew back. "I believe in freedom of choice. That a woman's body is hers. And if she can't be a good mother to her child, she'd be wise not to bring her baby into the world."

Allessandra shook her head, and Annie felt she was about to mouth "tsk-tsk" the way she was looking at her. Annie didn't discuss this subject with many people, and certainly never talked about it with a teenager.

"That's why there's such a thing as adoption, Annie. Unwanted children can have a place to go where they'll be loved and taken care of, if the birth mother can't have her own baby."

Annie nodded. "I understand your point."

"And by that you mean what? That you agree with me?"

Annie sighed. "No. It's not always so easy. Every situation's unique. You can't box everything up and tie it with a perfect little bow. It's not that simple."

"To me it is." Allessandra stared at Annie pointedly. "What if your situation had been different for some reason and you aborted Rafe?"

"I understand what you're trying to say, but that doesn't mean I agree with you."

She threw her shovel to the ground and wiped her hands on the sides of her pants. "I gotta go."

"Okay. You probably shouldn't be on your feet so much in this hot sun anyway. Let me drive you home."

"No, I'll walk, thanks."

They collected the gardening tools and put them in the garage.

"I plan to go to the nursery tomorrow to pick up some tomato and zucchini plants. Would you like to go with me?"

"I don't think so. I might have to work at the market."

Annie stopped and touched her lightly on the arm. Allessandra turned in Annie's direction. "There's no reason we can't agree to disagree. I respect your opinion. Can't you respect mine?"

Allessandra stared at the ground. "I guess so. Just seems like you're suggesting I abort my baby."

"I most certainly am not saying that. I think it's extraordinarily unselfish of you to go through an entire pregnancy and have someone else adopt your child. I admire you, Honey."

She looked straight at Annie with misty eyes. "Thanks for saying that."

Annie tried a small smile. "See you tomorrow?"

"Yeah."

Allessandra walked down the driveway, looking a bit forlorn. Maybe her anger had more to do with her ambivalence about putting her child up for adoption than Annie's opinion concerning abortion.

That evening Annie found a Santa Barbara County phone book and searched for general contractors. The house needed painting and the very old garage needed to be fixed. There were two general contractors listed in Brandiss. Annie believed in supporting local businesses so she phoned the first number and left a message.

The second number was Prescott Beemiller. The phone rang several times before a deep male voice answered.

"Beemiller Construction".

"Hello, my name is Annie Davidson. I just bought a house at 1106 Ivy Place and I'm looking for someone to paint the outside, fix the garage, that sort of thing. Do you have time to take a look?"

"I think I've seen you around town once or twice, Mrs. Davidson. You moved here not too long ago, right?"

"Yes. My son and I moved here from the Bay Area."

"I just finished a job on Main Street, near the elementary school, in case you'd like to take a look-see, talk to the owner, ask him about my work."

"What's the address on Main Street?"

"1201 Main. The man's name is Louis Frankfurth."

"Thanks. I'll have to stop by. Would you be available to meet tomorrow morning, around ten o'clock, Mr. Beemiller?"

He laughed. "Call me Prescott."

Annie smiled. "Call me Annie."

"I'll see you tomorrow, Annie."

The next day at precisely ten a.m. there was a knock on the front door. Annie was in the kitchen making lemonade and quickly put the pitcher in her new refrigerator and walked down the hall to answer it.

The contractor was about Annie's age, early thirty's, short dark brown hair, long sideburns. He reached up and took off his sunglasses, Hazel eyes, long black lashes, straight nose, thick dark eyebrows, a solid chin.

Unlike Cameron's smooth, clean-shaven face, Prescott had that look, very popular these days, with the two-day stubble, mustache, goatee, and a little strip of hair right in the middle of his chin; a real tough-guy look without reaching the Hells Angel level.

There was something about the sideburns and goatee, or perhaps the black vest covering his clean white t-shirt, the chain dangling from the side pocket of his form-fitting jeans, or the black biker boots. They all added up to a very impressive package, a real manly man.

Annie's heart did a little pitter-pat that she hoped hadn't caused her to blush.

"Good morning, Annie." He smiled, and his dark mustache enhanced the whiteness of his straight teeth.

Annie's smile widened. "Good morning, Prescott. You're right on time. Would you like to look at the outside of the house first?"

He nodded. "I'll take measurements, see how the previous paint job is holding up, and then we can talk possible numbers. I'll want to work up a formal bid. I could get that to you by tomorrow."

"Sounds fine to me." She opened the screen door and joined him on the porch.

They walked around the house and he pointed out areas more weather-beaten than others and spots that needed repair. They returned to the front yard and walked inside the house, into the front room.

"Make yourself comfortable," Annie said and gestured toward the couch.

"Thanks." He rubbed his hand along the armrest. "This is a beautiful piece. An heirloom?"

Annie sat across from him on an old cedar chest that needed to be refinished. "I got that from my mom. It was in storage when we lived up north. It didn't match the modern decor of our home, but I think it blends in perfectly in this house."

He bent toward her and rubbed his hand along the edge of the love chest she was sitting on, nodding. "With a little work, this piece could be restored."

"You do that sort of work, too?"

He shrugged. "More of a hobby than anything. Can't make enough money doing it for a living."

Annie nodded, loving the deep timber of his voice. "So, are you interested in taking on this project? Do you have time?"

He sat back and perused the notes on his clipboard. "What I'll do is work up a few different bids and their respective prices. I have a program on my computer at home. I just plug in the measurements and it does the calculations for me. I'll call you and we'll set up a time to go over it. That okay?"

Annie nodded. "Sounds good."

He stood to leave and they shook hands, his grip firm. His large hands enveloped hers like a glove. Their eyes met for a wisp of a second and Annie felt a zinging spark.

She unclasped her hand as if she'd been bitten and instantly dropped her gaze, turned and walked to the front door, the heavy steps of his boots clomping behind her. She pushed the screen door open and he walked out and turned around to face her.

"I'll call you," he said.

She couldn't meet his gaze but let the screen door close as she said a quick, "Thank you."

Annie returned to the front room and sat on the couch. It was still warm from where he'd been only moments before. His truck's engine started and rumbled down the street. She laid her head on the back of the couch, slid her fingers along the edge of the wood where he'd rested his arms. A tingle of excitement hummed inside her.

What was going on?

CHAPTER NINE

Later that evening Rafe was doing homework while Annie worked on a dot-to-dot book that she'd discovered several years ago. David Kalvitis created them for adults and many pictures had over a thousand dots. The puzzles were extraordinarily complicated in their intricate designs.

The unusual peace and quiet of Ivy Place enveloped her. Perhaps it was like this everywhere in the sleepy town of Brandiss, but Annie had never lived in a small town. Whether morning, noon, or night, she cherished the silence.

As the sunset's colors seeped through the front room windows, the intermittent cooing of a dove's call sounded and Annie let her mind wander.

And who popped into her mind? Prescott Beemiller.

She gave her head a little shake and tried again to make her mind blank, as she learned in yoga class. But each time, her thoughts meandered back to Prescott; his long legs as he walked around the house, his large hands pulling out the measuring tape, the way his pants hugged his thighs as he bent down to check the foundation.

Oh, hell. It was time to have dessert. Maybe she'd stop thinking about him if she ate some ice cream.

That night, after reading for a half hour, Annie went to sleep at ten o'clock. A little after midnight she awoke with a start. She lay there and tried to figure out if a sound had awakened her, or maybe it had been a dream. She sat up and listened with her eyes closed, but heard nothing but silence.

She slipped her feet into the pink fleece slippers she kept beside her bed. Maybe it would calm her mind if she made sure Rafe was asleep and hadn't gotten out of bed for some reason. She reached his door and peered around the corner. He was sleeping soundly. She tiptoed over to the side of his bed and pulled up his Star Trek comforter, which had slid part way onto the floor.

She headed downstairs and checked the front and back doors on her way to the kitchen to get a glass of water. As she suspected, both doors were solidly locked. It was silent throughout the house. Nothing appeared out of place.

She couldn't figure out what had awakened her. Perhaps it had been a bad dream after all. Or her subconscious obsessing over Prescott, anxiety building with anticipation of his call. Which, of course, made her think of Cameron.

Was she feeling guilty, dreaming about another man?

The next day Prescott called and came over soon afterward. Annie ushered him into the front room where he took a seat on the couch.

"Here's the estimate." He handed the bid to her. "It's a line by line explanation of what you want done and how much it'll cost." He stood to leave, tapping the front sheet of his copy with a pencil. "These figures could be less, or higher, depending on the cost of materials at the time of purchase, or if you want to go more high-end. Why don't you take some time to study it? I'll wait for your call. Any questions you might have, concerns, or whatever, I'd be happy to talk about."

After Cameron's death, Annie was left financially well-off. If she spent her money wisely, she wouldn't need to work outside of the home while Rafe was growing up, or maybe ever again. Cam had planned for their future more thoroughly than she was aware and with the sale of Davidson Construction Annie had more money than she'd ever imagined.

Annie stood and placed her hand on Prescott's forearm to stop him from walking away. "Your bid is more than fair. I spoke with Mr. Frankfurth over on Main Street and he couldn't have praised you more highly. Whenever you could start work here is fine."

He smiled and ducked his head a bit. "Thank you, Annie. This is a big job and I appreciate your trusting me to take it on, especially since you're new to this town."

They shook hands, and Annie walked him to the door and said good-bye.

He was personable, easy to talk with, and she liked the way he explained things without being condescending or sexist. He cared about what he was taking on. It wasn't just another project he could add to his belt. That was refreshing and she looked forward to having him around.

That evening Annie was helping Rafe with his spelling words when the phone rang. She grabbed the wireless handset, pleasantly surprised to hear a familiar voice on the line.

"Annie, this is Prescott. I've rearranged my schedule. I can start tomorrow, if that's okay."

She felt a small flutter in her chest. "You didn't have to do that. There's nothing here that can't wait."

He chuckled and Annie could almost see that smile, his dark mustache twitching upward at the sides, those hazel eyes of his squinting.

"Not a problem, Annie. I have a buddy who's a bit down on his luck right now. He could use the money, so I referred a couple of my clients to him. That way, he won't have to move back with his folks, and I get started on your house right away. It's a win-win situation."

What a guy! Handsome and smart as well. "I appreciate your doing that. I'll see you tomorrow."

When she hung up the phone, Annie explained to Rafe about Prescott and the work he'd be doing on their house, to keep him apprised of who would be in and out of their home for what might turn out to be months.

Rafe had loved watching his father work around the house. He'd beg Cameron to allow him on the job site as well, so he could watch the homes being built. For Cam and Rafe, the construction of a house was like a puzzle you assembled. The process was the fun part.

Rafe was growing like a weed and would be eleven years old in October. He sprouted two inches since the beginning of the year and his pants were starting to look like "floods." They had to go shopping soon. However, since arriving in Brandiss, buying the house, enrolling Rafe in school, and hiring Allessandra and Prescott, she'd been too busy.

Annie discovered that she rarely used her car. It was easy to walk everywhere in Brandiss, and she'd grown tired of the zoom-zoom pace of the Bay Area. Brandiss was much less stressful, more the type of life she wanted for herself and her son.

Annie remembered playing hide-and-go-seek outside with her friends after dark when she was growing up, walking to school and back each day with her next door neighbor David, stomping on the dead leaves that had fallen off the trees and loving the sound of their crackling under her feet.

She hadn't a care in the world back then and wanted that for Rafe. Cameron and Annie had spoken often of moving to a smaller city but that never happened. However, Annie was determined to make it happen for Rafe in Brandiss.

The next day, after dropping Rafe off at school, she returned to find a large white Chevy truck, buffed to a shine, parked in her driveway. Prescott was unloading scaffolding from the back of the long bed.

"Good morning," Annie said and started up the walkway toward the front door.

"Morning, Annie. Another gorgeous day in Brandiss."

"I haven't seen anything but beautiful weather since we got here."

He stood with his hands tucked into his back pockets. "Our winters aren't too bad either. It rarely drops below thirty-five degrees and that happens around Christmas time, when you kind of want it to be a little on the cold side anyway."

"The climate in Sausalito is pretty moderate. Most of the time I never had to even pull out my winter coat. I don't care for extreme temperatures, which is why I've always lived along the coast."

"I remember you said you're from the Bay Area. Your son would probably love it if we had one of our freak snow storms. I could help him build a snow man in the front yard."

Annie was surprised to hear him volunteer. Did he have children of his own? "Rafe would love that."

With that, Annie popped into the house to call Allessandra, to see if she was feeling better. Allessandra had been tired lately, but she said she'd join Annie in the garden.

Later, when Allessandra arrived, Annie heard the two of them laughing and talking together in the back yard. Given the number of people who lived in Brandiss, Annie shouldn't have been surprised. Allessandra had explained that she'd known Prescott most of her life so they had more than a passing acquaintance.

This was new to Annie, the close friendships that formed between people in small towns. The anonymity one has living in a big city can be a blessing when you don't want everyone to get into your business. Yet, the comfort of being surrounded by those who are there for you, wanting to help you out, made Annie feel less lonely.

When they sat at the kitchen table that afternoon to take a break, Allessandra's expression turned serious. "I've been thinking about this whole adoption thing."

Annie nodded. "It's a hard decision to have to make."

"I talked with a nurse practitioner at my gynecologist's office? She gave me a bunch of pamphlets about adoption, closed adoptions, open adoptions, that sort of thing... " She took her finger and slid it round and round the rim of her glass of tea.

"Anyway, a few days ago I called one of the hotlines where they give you free legal advice if you can't afford an attorney. The dude told me that in California, it's totally my decision." She slanted her gaze sideways and looked at Annie.

"One of Rafe's former classmates was adopted. The mother and I spoke a few times over the course of the school year about the process she went through to adopt her little girl Melanie, but I still don't know much about it."

"Well, I found out I get to choose who I want to be the new mom." Allessandra paused and sat up straight, her long blonde ponytail flopped over her shoulder.

"You have time to think about this, Allessandra. And even if you're not sure, don't you have several months after the adoptive parents take the baby to change your mind?"

"Yeah. The guy said I can pretty much decide how long I have to change my mind, as long as everybody agrees to it. In California the birth mother can consent to give up her baby any time after the baby's born. That's the law. So I could make it a month or six months or whatever to make my final decision to give the baby up for adoption, if I wanted to wait that long. Or he said I could waive any waiting period too. It'd be up to me mostly, if I went through an attorney and it was all written up legal and stuff." She exhaled a long breath of air and looked up at the ceiling.

Annie reached out and gave her hand a squeeze. "You'll figure it out."

She took a sip of tea and stared at Annie for a few seconds. "Well, the thing is... "

"Mmm?" Annie raised her eyebrows. What was on Allessandra's mind?

"Would you be interested in having my baby? I mean, not having it, like, of course, I'm the one who's having it. But, I mean, would you want it? Like, would you want to adopt my baby?"

Annie covered her mouth with her hand, eyes wide.

"Annie?" Allessandra tapped Annie on the arm.

"Do you know what you're asking? You... you've only known me a short while."

"I know. But we've spent a bunch of time together. I feel like I know you already. I want the baby to have a family, Annie, and you already have Rafe. I know your husband's dead but one of these days you'll marry somebody else. Then the baby would have a dad, too."

Luckily, Annie was sitting, because otherwise she would have dropped to her knees. She drew in a deep breath to calm her nerves and still her heartbeat. "You're not serious." She placed her hand on her chest. Her heart thrummed under her palm. "You haven't thought this through."

Allessandra rolled her eyes. "Yes, I have. Thought it through, I mean. And I want you to be my baby's mom."

Annie shook her head in disbelief.

"Look," Allessandra continued and leaned toward Annie. "My mom and dad are both dead. I don't have any brothers and sisters. Shit, I don't have anyone at all except for my cousin Stacey and my Aunt Barb. And Aunt Barb doesn't want a baby around at her age. She's had this boyfriend for, like, five years and they're planning to drive around the country after Stacey graduates."

Allessandra blew out a puff of air. "I wanna travel. When I turn eighteen, I'll have all the money in my trust fund. Living with Aunt Barb was gonna be temporary anyways. I've always wanted to get outta Brandiss. This would be perfect if you adopted my baby."

"I don't know what to say," Annie choked out. "I'm honored you'd consider me to adopt your child. I know there are attorneys who specialize in open adoptions. He or she could help you select an appropriate couple."

"That sorta thing just seems weird to me, Annie. Looking

through applications? Like the people are applying for a job at the grocery store or something? And what am I gonna do, interview them? Sounds kinda corny to me. At least I know you. I've seen how you really are. And I like you. Those other people would be trying to impress me with how perfect they'd be as parents for my baby. How phony is that?"

"Well, I don't know what to say. I mean, if you're serious, I'll think about it. But I'll have to talk it over with Rafe."

She grinned. "Oh, I'm serious." She stood. "But, yeah, talk to Rafe about it. That's a good idea." She waved goodbye, saying over her shoulder, "Take as much time as you need."

"See you tomorrow," Annie murmured to her departing figure.

CHAPTER TEN

That evening after dinner, Rafe waved his hand in front of Annie's face. "Hel-lo. Mom, you in there?"

"Sorry," Annie said and shook her head. "I was just thinking about Allessandra."

"She told me her baby's probably gonna be born on St. Patrick's Day."

"Pretty exciting stuff, huh?" Annie gazed out the window to the backyard. "I remember how your father and I felt before you were born. We counted down the months, and then the weeks and days. After you were born we couldn't take our eyes off you. Your dad took a whole month off work to help take care of you." She turned her gaze in his direction. "Of course, you can't remember that, but I have pictures. And as soon as I find that box, we'll look at them."

"Yeah. I don't remember being a baby."

She laughed. "Of course you don't. I don't think I ever talked to you about how you'd feel if you had a brother or sister."

"Some of my friends have little sisters and brothers, and they always tell me how they mess with their toys and barf on their shirts and stuff."

She nodded. "Well, babies sometimes complicate our lives. But having a brother or sister doesn't scare you, does it? Or make you sad about not being the only kid in the house?"

"No. I just wouldn't want anybody breaking my Nintendo. And I don't want to clean up baby barf." He stopped, an odd expression on his face. "Why are we talking about this?"

Annie stood and grabbed his hand. "Let's go out on the porch and sit outside for a while."

She needed those few moments. The old cliché about there being no manual on how to raise your kid kept popping up in her head.

They sat on the porch swing and Annie kicked her feet. A gentle breeze hit their faces as they rocked back and forth. She laid her head back and gazed up at the stars.

"Remember the little girl in your class last year who was adopted?"

"Melanie," he said.

"Yes. Well, yesterday Allessandra and I were talking and she's not going to keep her baby."

"I know. She told me she was gonna give it to someone who could take care of it better 'cause she doesn't have much money and she wants to travel around with Stacey."

Annie turned toward him. His legs didn't quite reach the porch floor and his dark hair fluffed up and down as they swung back and forth. "She wants to know if we'd adopt her baby."

His face revealed nothing though she knew this must be a shock to him.

"She didn't say that to me," he said.

"Well, she wanted to ask me first, I guess, because I'm the adult."

He jumped off the porch swing and stood in front of her.

"What did you tell her?"

Annie placed her feet on the porch to stop the swing and leaned toward him. "I didn't tell her anything, Rafe, except that you and I would have to talk about it."

Annie couldn't read his facial expression though his eyes appeared wide and unblinking. "Would you want to have a brother or sister?"

He shrugged.

"I've been thinking about this ever since Allessandra told me and you know what? I like having our little family, just you and I. Of course I still miss your father, but I'm just getting used to it being the two of us, ya' know?"

He sat on the deck in front of her and crossed his legs. "I miss him, too." He chewed on his thumbnail. "I get bored sometimes with nobody to play with."

"If we had a baby it would certainly take up a lot of my time. I would be busy feeding the baby and rocking it to sleep and just... it's a big job. And until the baby is older, you wouldn't be able to play with him or her."

"Were you gonna have another baby? I mean, if Daddy were still alive?"

She nodded. "We talked about it. We wanted you to have a brother or sister."

"So are you gonna tell Allessandra that you'll adopt her baby?"

"Rafe, Honey, you and I are a family, even though your dad isn't alive. We have to make this decision together. It's something both of us have to want or it shouldn't happen."

"Yeah."

"It would probably be a good idea for both of us to think about it for a while. How 'bout that?"

He nodded.

"There's another thing I have to tell you about, too. You know, if she gave us her baby to adopt, she has the right to change her mind. You and I would fall in love with the baby and if Allessandra wanted to take her baby back, we'd have to give the baby to her."

His eyebrows drew down in a vee. and he fiddled with his shoe lace. "That's sorta messed up." He paused and looked up at her. "You mean she could take the baby back, even if the baby's, like, two or three years old or something?"

She chuckled. "No, honey, that's not how it works. There are legal time limits. Let's say she'd have six months or something to change her mind. As an example, I mean. After that the baby would be ours forever. I don't know much about the adoption process. We'd all have to agree to this beforehand. I know it would break my heart if we had to give the baby back to her." She hugged him and kissed his soft cheek. "I think we should both think about this and talk about it later. And if you and I both want to do this, I'll tell her yes. Okay?"

"'Kay."

With that, they walked into the kitchen for a night time snack and to bed afterward.

The next morning Annie phoned Allessandra to see how she was feeling. She was doing well, so Annie invited her to stay for dinner after they finished gardening for the day.

Prescott was almost finished putting up the scaffolding and would soon be painting the front of the house. Annie walked up to where he was standing at the back of his truck, a hot latte in each hand.

"Do you drink coffee?" she asked and lifted one steaming cup in his direction.

"Are you kidding me? It's my drink of choice, especially on a cold morning like this one." He took the cup from her hands, brought it to his lips and took a few sips. "Thank you very much."

"You're very welcome. I have a wonderful espresso machine. If I don't get my daily fix, I'd have to enter rehab."

He laughed out loud. Something Annie hadn't heard in so long—the sound of a man's deep, throaty voice. Obviously, it had been way too long since she'd been around someone of the opposite sex.

He gestured toward the back yard. "You and Allessandra have done a great job on the garden."

She smiled and took another sip. "Thanks. She's been a big help. She told me she's known you since she was young. I like her. She seems like a good kid."

He nodded. "She is. This is a small town. People get to know a lot more about each other than when you live in a big city. She's had a rough time these last few years, what with her parents being killed, and then getting pregnant."

Annie cupped the hot latte in her hands, blowing along the rim of the mug. "I didn't grow up in a small place like this. In the past, I would have believed that people were just being nosey. But I've changed my mind. And you two have everything to do with opening my eyes about small town life. Thank you for that."

His hazel eyes locked onto hers. "You're welcome. With any luck, you'll love it here, too. But Allessandra wants out of Brandiss."

She nodded slowly. "Maybe there are just too many memories for her here. I sure understand that. She needs to get away, start somewhere new." She paused. "It worked for me." Suddenly feeling as if she was getting too personal, she shook her head, embarrassed at having revealed a bit too much. "I've gotta go. Sorry to have kept you from your work."

As she turned to leave, his hand gently covered her forearm. "You're not keeping me from my work, Annie. I'm allowed a coffee break, aren't I, boss?"

With a small grin, Annie backed away, letting his hand slip from her arm. "Of course you are. It's just... I have shopping to do. It's getting late, and Allessandra's coming over to help me. I'll see you later."

She gave him a quick wave and jogged up the front stairs to the house. She wanted to go to the open-air market, held on Main Street once a week, pick up some fruits for a salad, and vegetables for the lasagna. Then she'd stop by the supermarket for ice cream, pasta, and sourdough bread.

When Allessandra finished up later that day, she sat at the kitchen table, gazing out the window at the back yard while Rafe sat across from her doing his homework. Allessandra and Annie had made great headway in the garden and they'd almost finished planting the vegetables she'd purchased from the nursery.

Annie was checking the lasagna in the oven when someone knocked on the back door.

"Sorry to bother you," Prescott said, "but could I have a drink of water?"

The sun was directly hitting the side of the house where he was working. He'd removed his t-shirt and his chest hairs sparkled under a sheen of sweat.

His upper body was solid and fit... very fit. He had the naturally muscled torso a guy gets from hammering, lifting heavy equipment, lugging tools around every day.

His waist cut in enough to show he hadn't an ounce of fat around his belly; his pants hung low enough on his hips to reveal the deep vee of dark hair growing downward. Combined with the tan his face had acquired from working in the sun for several weeks, he looked like Adonis from a Greek movie.

Annie's tongue stuck to the roof of her mouth and she'd lost her voice. His eyebrows drew down in a vee. My God, she hadn't given him an answer!

"Oh. Yes. Sure. I'm sorry. Would you like to sit down while I get you something cold to drink?"

He pulled out a chair, spun it around, and straddled it. "Sure, I'll sit down for a little bit." He turned toward Allessandra. "How're you feeling? Bet you're looking forward to St. Pat's Day, huh?"

She slapped him lightly on the forearm. "You know it, Pres. I already don't fit in my skinny jeans. I don't like having a pot belly." She paused and looked at Annie. "In fact, I was hoping tonight I'd get Annie to give me an answer to the question I asked her the other night."

CHAPTER ELEVEN

Annie stared at Allessandra. "Could we talk about this, uh, alone, some other time?"

Allessandra glanced at Prescott. "I talked with Pres about this before I ever asked you, Annie. I wanted his input as, like, an adult."

A hot blush crawled up Annie's face, and she tried to busy herself getting plates down from the cabinet. "I didn't know. It's your decision and your baby. I assumed, obviously incorrectly, you hadn't spoken with anyone about this yet."

"So?" Allessandra asked.

Annie glanced over at Rafe then at Allessandra. "Rafe and I need more time to think about this. It would be best if we leave the discussion for another day."

Allessandra shrugged. "No problem." She grabbed the plates out of Annie's hands and began setting the table. "Can Pres eat dinner with us, too?"

Annie glanced from Prescott to Rafe and back at Prescott. "Would you like to stay for dinner, Prescott?" She handed him a glass of water. "Vegetable lasagna, fruit salad, French bread, two kinds of ice cream."

"Thank you." He took a moment before he answered. "I'd love to. Can I help out with anything?"

"No, thank you. It'll be about ten minutes before dinner's ready."

Prescott stood, drained his glass of water, and then turned toward Rafe. "Wanna play a little catch in the backyard before we eat?"

"Sure," Rafe said, a big smile on his face.

There hadn't been a male figure in Rafe's life since Cam's death. Annie felt guilty jumping on the dating band wagon, not ready to entertain the idea of allowing another man into her heart or her life. It had been inappropriate and way too early during the year and a half after Cam died.

After Allessandra set the table, Annie called out to Prescott and Rafe that dinner was ready, and they all sat down to eat. Rafe jabbered away with Prescott about school and basketball. He was having a meal with someone other than his mom and seemed to be enjoying it. It was obvious he missed the camaraderie of a family bigger than just he and his mom. Annie hadn't noticed how quiet it had been at meal time until tonight.

Prescott glanced up from his empty plate and wiped his mouth with a napkin. "This lasagna is great, Annie. And the fruit salad's delicious. Thank you for inviting me."

"You're welcome. Would you like some ice cream for dessert? Allessandra, how about you?"

Allessandra shook her head. "Sorry, guys, I'm stuffed. And I'm so tired, I'm afraid I'm gonna fall asleep at the table."

Prescott stood as Allessandra pushed her chair out. "Do you need a ride home?"

She shook her head. "No, but thanks anyway. Think I'll walk home. I need the exercise. The doctor said it's good for me." She glanced at Annie. "And good for the baby, too."

Prescott sat back down as she waved goodbye.

"Can I watch Nickelodeon, Mom? Spongebob's gonna start soon," Rafe said.

"Just put your plate in the sink first, Sweetie. You can have dessert later if you want."

He ran out of the kitchen, leaving Annie alone with Prescott.

"So, you talked with Allessandra about her wanting me to adopt her baby?" she asked.

"Yeah. I don't want you to feel like I've invaded your privacy. That's not the way it was. Allessandra and I have known each other for years. I've practically watched her grow up. She trusts me, Annie. She needed to talk to an adult, so I guess I was it."

"In your place, I would have done the same thing. It just surprised me to hear anyone knew about this. I'm glad she could go to you for advice, to get an adult's viewpoint." Annie glanced down into her glass of tea and toyed with the lemon slice. "I don't know you that well but her confidence in you... . Let's just say, I see you in a different light now."

He raised his eyebrows. "Wow. You thought I might be a serial killer before you found out she talked to me about the adoption?" He laughed and placed his fingers over her hand.

Annie's heart blipped erratically. She looked down at her hand, encased in his rather large grasp, and then up at him.

He unfurled his fingers from hers. "I guess I should go, Annie. Thanks again for dinner. I don't get many chances to eat a home-cooked meal."

She leaned back. "Do you have children, Prescott?"

His smile disappeared.

"I ask because you obviously helped Allessandra make her decision to put her baby up for adoption and... I was just wondering."

He leaned to the side, reached his hand into his back pocket and brought out a worn leather wallet. He placed it on the table in front of Annie, opened it, and pushed it toward her. "That was my wife Patti." He paused. "And my son, Dylan."

She looked at the photograph. "She's beautiful. And your little boy... he's about seven or eight months old? When was this photo taken?"

"He was eight months old then. About two years ago. At a park in Santa Barbara."

"You said she was you wife. So you're divorced?"

He touched the picture with his finger, his mouth set in a firm line. "She and Dylan disappeared. He just turned nine months old. The police investigated. The FBI was called in. I don't know if she left me or they were kidnapped. Either way, I don't have a wife or a son anymore."

"Oh, my God," she whispered. "That must have been terrible. What did you do?"

He cocked one eyebrow upward. "Do you really want to hear this?"

She nodded. "Yes, I do. If you're comfortable telling me."

He took a deep breath. "After they went missing I started drinking pretty heavily, lost some projects because I didn't show up, couldn't finish the work. The spouse is always the prime suspect and that was really hard to swallow. But the FBI announced they didn't believe I was involved."

He shook his head slowly from side to side. "About six months after they disappeared, I finally decided there wasn't a damn thing I could do about it. The police didn't have any leads. The FBI was clueless."

He stared up at the ceiling. "We owned a house in Carpinteria at the time, south of Santa Barbara. But I couldn't live there any longer... too many memories. I grew up in Brandiss. It was my home before I went to UC Santa Barbara. So I moved back here and started working on building my own business." His gaze met hers. "And here I am. I still miss them and always will. But I couldn't live my life seeing only the bottom of a bottle of Jack Daniels.

"I don't know if they're both dead, lying in some landfill. Or maybe they're alive. They could be living anywhere. I may never find out, which kills me. And at what point do I give up hoping they'll ever be found? Worst of all, Annie, I lost my son. I'll never stop dreaming I'll see him again."

She reached out and grasped his hand. "I am so sorry. I can't imagine what you've been through... what you're going through still."

He closed his wallet and stuffed it in his back pocket. "I better get going."

They stood at the same time, their bodies only inches away from each other. Their eyes met. Slowly, he lifted her chin with his finger and pressed his lips to hers. One small kiss. He dropped his hand and smiled. "I'll see you tomorrow, Annie."

"Yeah," she mumbled. "See you."

He turned and walked out the back door. His footsteps on the stairs echoed in the night's silence.

What just happened?

CHAPTER TWELVE

By the end of the week, Prescott would start on the back of the house. Annie wanted to put a small fence around the garden to save it from getting stepped on by Rafe and his buddies, who often played in the backyard. She was in the process of taking measurements when footsteps echoed behind her.

She turned around to see Prescott, a serious expression on his face. "What's the matter?" she said.

"I just drove by Allessandra's place. Saw an ambulance leaving the house."

She grabbed onto his arm for support, suddenly light-headed.

"It could be Stacey," he said, "or Barb, or a neighbor. I don't know."

She rushed up the back stairs, Prescott close at her heels, raced to the phone in the kitchen and punched in Barb's number. After several rings, the answering machine picked up. She slammed down the phone.

"Try again," Prescott urged.

This time a woman picked up immediately. "This is Annie Davidson. Is this Barb?"

"Yes, this is Barb. Hello, Annie."

"Prescott saw an ambulance in front of your house just a while ago. Is Allessandra alright?"

"When she woke up this morning, she was cramping and bleeding slightly."

Annie gasped, her heart in her throat. "Blood? Is she alright?"

"I don't know. I thought it was best to call an ambulance instead of driving her there myself. They took her to Sea Cliff Memorial Hospital."

"Thanks, Barb. I'm leaving right way."

"Stacey's on her way home from work. She and I will be heading to the hospital soon. Maybe we'll see you there."

They ended the call and Annie turned to Prescott. "I'd like to go to the hospital."

"I'll drive."

"I have to arrange for someone to pick Rafe up from school." She took a deep breath and tried not to cry. "I feel so bad for her. Even though she doesn't want to keep her baby, I know she doesn't want to lose the baby like this."

Prescott wrapped Annie in his arms, his chin resting on the crown of her head. "Do you have someone to pick up Rafe?"

"I'll ask Abby. She's taken care of him in the past." She called Abby, arranged for her to take care of Rafe then grabbed her purse.

They rushed out to Prescott's truck and within moments were on their way. Annie laid her head back, tilted the seat to a more reclined position, and closed her eyes. Prescott's warm hand covered hers and she intertwined her fingers with his.

"She's young and healthy—two big things in her favor, Annie. Don't get too upset until we find out what's really going on."

"It's not just that. This will be the first time I've been in a hospital since my husband's death two years ago."

He squeezed her hand and the warmth took the chill off her heart. "What happened?"

"A car accident. He died in the hospital several hours later." Annie tightened her grip on his hand, needing to feel close to someone right now. It had been so long since she'd reached out to anyone for solace.

He pulled his hand away and pushed a button on the car stereo. A few seconds later the soft notes of one of Annie's favorite songs floated through the truck's interior—the soundtrack from the movie *Gladiator*.

She opened her eyes and stared at his profile until he shot a quick glance in her direction. "What's wrong?" he asked. "You hated the movie and the song reminds you of the bloody battles in the film?" He reached over to eject the CD.

She softly placed her hand on his wrist. Their gazes connected for a second, and he let his arm drop down on the console between them.

"*Gladiator* is my favorite movie," Annie said. "I don't know anyone else who likes the film as much as I do. I cry every time I see it. You remember at the end when Maximus dies and finally gets to be with his wife and little boy in the afterlife? I swear, it gets to me each time I watch it."

He smiled. "I've seen the film about ten times."

Annie shut her eyes again and grinned. Sometimes something special happens between two people and, at that moment, she felt something just had.

It took forty-five minutes to get to Sea Cliff Memorial Hospital. They passed through the front doors to the lobby and Prescott waited for the receptionist to look up from her computer terminal. "Has Allessandra Dawson been admitted?"

The young girl typed in the information, before she pointed behind her. "Second floor. Room 201. Take the elevator and exit toward your left."

Annie walked as if through quicksand toward the bank of elevators, clutching Prescott's hand. Suddenly he stopped, pulling her up short.

"What is it?" she asked, out of breath.

He grabbed her other hand and turned her to face him. "I can't imagine how hard this must be for you. Like a bad walk down memory lane. But you have a friend here." He smiled. "You'll get through this."

Annie stared up at him, his face etched in worry. "You're right." She took a deep breath, tried to slow her heart rate.

"Take another one," he urged.

She closed her eyes and took another big gulp of air. Her chest tightened. "It's just... I equate hospitals with death. I can't help it. And now with Allessandra here, giving up her baby for adoption. That's hard enough, but if the baby doesn't survive, how can a young girl recover from such a tragedy?"

He folded her in his arms and she rested her head on his chest. His heart beat through his shirt, comforting her with its rhythm.

"We'll be there for her no matter what happens," he whispered.

Her heart lodged in her throat. "But if the baby dies... "

He pulled her away gently, looked her in the eyes. "That's out of our hands. She's done everything right during this pregnancy. There's nothing she could have done differently." He paused. "Now let's go up there." He gave her hands a tight squeeze.

She smiled. It had been a long time since she'd leaned on anyone. They walked side by side, holding hands, and took the elevator to the second floor, where the on-duty nurse pointed them toward Room 201.

When Allessandra glanced up from an empty lunch tray and smiled, Annie knew everything was going to be alright. "Hey," she said, her eyes focused on their clasped hands as Annie and Prescott rounded the corner.

"How are you?" Annie asked. "How's the baby?"

"We're both fine," Allessandra said, her face pink and glowing. "The doctor said it's not unusual to have a small amount of bleeding 'cause it's my first pregnancy. But I shouldn't be standing at the register in the market all day long, so there goes my travel money. But it's okay if I, like, sit on one of those cushion things and do some gardening."

All the air in Annie's lungs swooshed out. It felt as though she'd been holding her breath since she'd left Brandiss. She sat beside Allessandra on the hospital bed and hugged her. "I'm relieved you and the baby are going to be okay, Honey."

Allessandra leaned back on the pillows. "I'd be lying if I didn't admit that losing this baby would make my life a helluva lot easier. But I wanna give this baby to you and Rafe, Annie. I want you to be the mom this baby deserves."

Tears slid down Annie's face. "We'll talk about this at another time, Honey. Now, when can we take you home?"

"Tomorrow morning. Probably around eleven. But Stacey and Barb can probably pick me up. They'll be here soon and I can ask 'em."

Annie glanced at Prescott and he walked over and gave her a quick hug. "We'll pick you up."

"Thanks for coming." Allessandra wiggled her fingers at them. "Love you guys."

"We love you, too," Prescott answered and gave Allessandra another quick hug.

Annie and Prescott said good-bye and slowly walked to the parking lot.

"Well, that was a relief," he said, when they got in the truck. "Do you want to call Abby, tell her we'll be home soon? Or would you like to stop and get something to eat first?"

She reached over and took his hand. "Thank you for driving me. It sounds like she'll be okay. But being in the hospital... ."

"You did good." He pulled onto the highway, merged into traffic, and then glanced in her direction, his eyebrows drawn together. "I care about you, Annie."

As Annie's Nana used to say, "You could have knocked me over with a feather."

"I want to get to know you better," he added.

"Oh," she whispered.

He turned for a second in her direction. "Talk to me, Annie."

She stared out the side window. Cows grazed and the tree leaves blew in the wind.

She turned toward him, his profile rigid. "You're the first man I've spent more than a few minutes with since Cam died. I'm not sure how I feel. Plus I'm overwhelmed with this whole adoption thing."

She sighed and laid her head back. "I still feel married to Cam, so there's a part of me that's filled with guilt. But, intellectually, I know that's not true. Sometimes I wake up at night and I think he's lying there next to me. Then it hits me like a slap in the face. He's never coming back." Tears slipped down her cheeks. Hadn't she cried enough tears over Cam months ago to last her a lifetime? "But I don't want you to go away, Pres. I care about you, too."

He nodded. "Okay. I understand. How 'bout this?" He paused, looking pensive. "You let me hang around and get to know you better. Then we'll see where this takes us."

He slowed down behind a line of cars waiting for a herd of cows to cross the road. He pulled to a stop, and then turned toward her. "Take some time to sort out your feelings about the adoption, and my interest in you. After you do that, look around. I'll be there, waiting."

He eased the truck forward again. The cows had made it safely to the other side. Annie shut her eyes for a few minutes, not intending to fall asleep. But the next time she opened them, they were sitting in his truck, in front of a house on a street she'd never seen before.

CHAPTER THIRTEEN

Annie sat up and glanced out the window, confused and unsettled. She jumped when she felt a hand grasp hers. She turned to her left and tried to focus. Prescott leaned over the console, watching her.

"You awake?" he whispered.

She cleared her throat and sat up straight. "Uh, yeah. Where are we?"

"In front of my house. It's seven o'clock. If Rafe's already eaten and if you want to, we could call Abby, see if she minds having him stay with her. Instead of taking you out to dinner, I could cook for you."

Annie immediately felt hesitant about his invitation. Did he assume she was staying the night? Because that wasn't going to happen anytime soon. But maybe he was hopeful.

Well, no one had ever called her shy. She was poised to launch into a grandiose explanation, when he squeezed her hand to get her attention.

"Annie, I'm not asking you to sleep with me. We don't know each other well enough to take that step. I'm asking if I can cook you dinner. That doesn't mean I expect a damn thing from you in return. All right?"

"Yeah, sure," Annie said, feeling like a teenager.

"You and I have had a long day. Rafe is safe with Abby. I have everything to make a nice dinner right here at my house, so why not? I'll drive you home afterward and we'll pick up Rafe on the way."

"Okay," she said, sure that relief showed on her face. "I'd like that very much. Thank you."

He walked around to her side of the truck, opened the door to help her jump down to the sidewalk, and she followed him to the front of his house.

It was an older home, like Annie's. The front garden looked like something from *Sunset Magazine*. Gleaming dark and smooth in the moonlight, redwood fencing surrounded the house on both sides. Malibu lights glowed in the yard along the path leading to the front door.

Prescott reached into his pocket for his keys, opened the door, and they walked through the foyer into the front room. The interior design whispered comfort, warmth, and beauty, with lovely antique couches and deep-seated chairs with lots of pillows.

Annie sat on the couch and Prescott excused himself to start cooking in the kitchen that was connected to the front room by an arched doorway. She pulled off her shoes and stretched out her legs.

"The lasagna the other night was vegetarian," he called from the kitchen. "You don't eat meat?"

"Not in years," she answered, "but, believe me, I eat whatever side dishes you fix to go with the main course. Don't go out of your way to prepare something special for me."

"How about a vegetable and tomato mixture over rice? It's one of the few dishes I make that's edible."

"Sounds great. I'm sure I'll love it."

"All right. Won't take me long. Relax. Would you like me to light a fire for you while you're waiting?"

"I'm fine. In fact, I'm more than fine," she said, snuggling down amongst the pillows. "It's so comfortable in here. I love the way you've decorated your home."

"It's taken me years to get this far, believe me. I bought this house when it was cheap, needed work. I was in the remodeling business anyway, so I jumped on it. Now I can sit back and enjoy."

Annie felt too wound up to just lie on the couch. Her nap in the truck had renewed her energy, and knowing Allessandra was okay had lifted her spirits. She jumped up and joined him in the kitchen.

"Let me help you with dinner, Prescott. Where are we eating?"

He lifted the lid of the pot on the stove, took a peak, and turned toward her. "Are you sure you wouldn't rather take it easy, lie on the couch with your feet up?"

She shook her head.

"All right," he said. "It's much nicer in the kitchen than the formal dining room. Do you mind?"

"No, not at all. I'll set the table. Let me go wash up first."

Annie took advantage of the beautifully appointed bathroom down the hall. It had a claw-foot tub, pull-chain toilet, and big fluffy towels hung from oak towel bars.

When she came out, she noticed a picture on a side table in the hall of an attractive woman holding a baby in her arms, with a backdrop of low-hanging willow trees near a river. She picked it up to take a better look and felt Prescott's hand on her back.

"Patti and Dylan?" she said.

"Yeah." He took her hand and led her back into the kitchen.

After setting the table, he placed several covered dishes between them. They took turns serving themselves and began eating. A CD of Vivaldi's Four Seasons hummed in the background.

"Something's been eating at me, Prescott."

"What's up?"

She stared into his eyes. "You're a married man."

He nodded. "I am. I retained an attorney a couple of weeks ago after I spoke with the FBI about their ongoing search. They haven't turned up a damn thing. And it's been over two years."

"What can an attorney do that the FBI hasn't already done as far as finding your wife and son?"

He wiped his mouth with a napkin. "I need to get a service by publication."

"What's that?"

"My attorney has a private investigator who does a meticulous search for Patti before I publish my intent to divorce her in the local newspapers. He has to search for her in telephone directories in cities where she might be living, get in touch with her relatives, check the department of motor vehicles, prisons, police departments. And all of this has to be documented in detailed records to show the judge I've done everything possible to locate her."

"Sounds like he's doing everything the FBI and police should have already done, though."

"I agree. But this has everything to do with due diligence and getting a divorce." He blew out an exaggerated breath. "Here's how it works. After we turn over those search records to the judge, and if the judge orders me to carry out the service by publication, he'll decide where and how often I have to publish the notice in the newspapers. Most courts require the notice to be published for four to six continuous weeks, stating I'm suing Patti for dissolution of marriage."

He took a sip of water, placed the glass back on the table and turned it round and round several times. "Then, I have to file a sworn statement with the Clerk of the Court stating I've tried to find her but haven't been able to, and list the methods I've used with the records to back it up. That's where the private investigator comes in."

He took a deep breath. "Then I file an affidavit of publication with the court from the newspapers verifying I've published the notices for the set amount of time. And then the judge will, hopefully, proceed with the divorce."

Annie stared at him, shaking her head. "That's unbelievable. How long does all this take?"

"No telling, really, because you want the P.I. to do a thorough job or else your request will be denied. And I'll have wasted literally thousands of dollars on attorney fees and be in the same spot I'm in now."

She nodded. "Which is pretty much limbo."

"Correct. You really don't want to rush something like this. Plus, while the P.I. is searching, he could find a clue to their disappearance that the FBI and police didn't."

"You're doing everything you can, Prescott, with the attorney, the P.I., the FBI, and the police. If nothing shows up you'll know you've done everything possible to find them. What more can you do?"

"I need to move forward. I didn't want to proceed with a divorce before this time because I... " He stalled, his mouth working back and forth.

"You weren't ready to face the fact you'll never see her again?"

He nodded. "That... and admitting I won't ever see my son again. That hurts the most."

"Rips you apart, doesn't it?"

"And you know what else made me want to move on?"

Annie shook her head. "What?"

"When I met you, Annie, I realized I could feel something for another woman."

A hot blush crept up her neck to her face and she dipped her head. "I have no idea how you must feel after losing your wife and son. You're a good man, kind, caring, and hard-working. And my losing Cameron is completely different than what you had taken from you. But I understand emotional pain. And you're still hurting. It may always be painful for you."

Annie fiddled with the salt shaker on the table. "Sometimes I think I'll never get over the loss, but I hope to move forward again, too. Otherwise, I run the risk of falling back into that black hole, somewhere I really don't want to go." She looked up at him. "I care about you, Prescott. And I think there could be an us, if we both want it to happen. But we both know we've got to take this slowly."

A little half-smile graced his lips. "It's no surprise I'm falling for you, Annie Davidson." He placed his hand over hers, rubbing his thumb along her knuckles. "I don't want to go too fast, either, and I don't want to scare you away. Just please don't run from me. Everyone deals with loss in different ways, in different time frames. And if I have to wait, well, you're worth waiting for."

It seemed like a lifetime had passed since she'd heard words like that, and her heart beat hard beneath her ribs.

He pushed his chair back and stood. "It's nine o'clock. I think I should take you home. You must be exhausted. Do you want to call Abby and see about picking up Rafe on the way home?"

"That's a good idea. And thanks for fixing me dinner and going with me to the hospital today. I really appreciate it." She phoned Abby before they drove to the Inn at the Wayside and picked up Rafe.

After Prescott dropped them off she fell into bed, exhausted.

CHAPTER FOURTEEN

Annie stood next to an open grave in a cemetery. She'd been there before. Hundreds, maybe thousands of gravestones, as far as the eye can see. She looked to the left of the grave and could make out the names on the head stones. One had her mother's name on it and next to it, her father's.

Nothing identified the grave in front of her. There was no headstone. She glanced down, and her hand covered a smaller hand. Glancing over, she saw it was Rafe, and he's crying. She touched her face and felt tears there too. Taking a few steps forward, she looked down and saw a casket, clods of dirt strewn over the top.

She glanced around and there were thirty or forty people standing around her, their faces blurred. She wasn't able to identify anyone. She looked at her other hand. Unfolding her fingers, she saw a clump of dirt, damp and soft, not sure what she's supposed to do with it.

She had the impression people were waiting for her to do something, so she tossed the dirt and watched it splash silently on top of the casket, little pieces spraying over the edges.

She took a few steps back. She heard footsteps coming from behind her. Raising her head, she saw a man's silhouette, his face a blur. He took her hand and gently led her from the gravesite, away from the cemetery. They walked out the front gates together, with Rafe still grasping her other hand.

* * * *

Annie turned over and looked at the clock. Six a.m., and the music channel was playing a soft classical song. Time to get up.

Over breakfast, she talked with Rafe about Allessandra, allaying any fears he may have had about her visit to the hospital. After dropping him off at school, Annie took a short bike ride, feeling groggy after her dream, wanting to sweep away the cobwebs.

The sun had just shown its face above the clouds and she pedaled as fast as she could down Main Street to Brandiss Park and back. By the time she arrived home, she had enough time to take a shower, put on makeup and get dressed before Prescott arrived.

The doorbell chimed and she grabbed her pink sweatshirt and headed for the front door. Prescott was dressed in distressed jeans, a black polo shirt, and the requisite black biker boots. He'd gotten a haircut and his mustache and goatee were freshly trimmed. He looked so handsome.

The drive went by in a flash and they arrived promptly at eleven o'clock as Allessandra was pulling on her sweater. A woman in her early fifties stood next to her.

"Hi, you two," Allessandra said, a huge grin on her face. "Barb, this is Annie and you already know Prescott. Barb's on her way to Santa Barbara and stopped here first to sign the release papers."

"That's right," Annie said. "You're not eighteen yet." She reached out her hand to Barb. "Nice to meet you."

Barb stared at Annie for a few seconds, as though thinking about something, and then took hold of her hand. "It's nice to meet you, too, Annie." She paused. "I've heard a lot about you and your son Rafe."

Annie glanced over at Allessandra. "My son and I are very fond of Allessandra. She's a good worker. I guess you're going to have to take it easy from now on though. Are you going to give your notice at the supermarket?"

"Yeah, I better call today," she said.

Annie sat next to Allessandra. "I don't want you over-exerting yourself, so perhaps you should retire from working in my backyard, too."

"I need the money, Annie," she said. "There's a big difference between standing all day and sitting on the ground pulling weeds." She patted her stomach. "I'll need to buy some bigger shirts to cover my huge-ass belly soon."

Barb patted Allessandra on the shoulder. "Well, if you hadn't gotten pregnant you wouldn't have to earn extra money for maternity clothes."

Silence descended on the room like a dark curtain. Annie could hear the birds chirping outside, cars passing by. She placed her hand on Allessandra's arm and glanced at Prescott. "We should go."

Allessandra reached up and touched Annie's hand. "Thanks for picking me up today. And can Stacey ride back with us, too?

Annie nodded. "Of course."

"Thanks for taking the two of them home," Barb said. "This works out perfect for me because I have some errands to do."

"It's no problem at all, Barb," Annie said. "We're glad to do it. Ready to go?"

Allessandra's expression had turned serious and she avoided looking at Annie. "Yeah. Let's get outta here."

They waited for Barb to sign the release papers, said good-bye to her and piled into the truck and entered Brandiss a little after noon. They brought Allessandra's things inside Barb's house, settled her in front of the television with Stacey, and then returned to the truck.

"That was odd," Annie said. "Back at the hospital, when Barb made that comment to Allessandra about getting pregnant."

Prescott gave her a brief look as he backed out of the driveway. "I don't know Barb that well. Maybe it's typical of the way she and Allessandra interact. I wouldn't make a lot out of it. Allessandra's there for the short term anyway, and lucky to have a place to live."

Annie gazed out the side window. "It just felt awkward. Blaming Allessandra for getting pregnant when she's so far along seems rather insensitive, and she doesn't need that right now. Not after having the scare she had yesterday."

"You've got a point. It'll all be over for her pretty soon. She'll be as free as a bird and can travel to wherever she wants. I think she and Stacey have been making plans."

Annie stared at him as he pulled up in front of her house. "Did she say that to you? That she and Stacey are leaving right after the birth?"

"She's hoping you'll give her your answer soon, Annie."

"And if I don't say yes?"

"She'll find an attorney to handle the adoption or talk to Child Protective Services."

"And if Rafe and I want to adopt her baby, she's just going to leave right away?"

"That's the plan. She'll be eighteen soon and Barb won't be in control of her inheritance any more. She wants to travel and so does Stacey."

"Barb won't like it if they both drop out of high school early." She grabbed the door handle.

"Wait, Annie." He put his hand on her arm. "I promise not to say anything to her, but have you made a decision yet?"

"You know, Cam and I always wanted to have more children. In a way this is a golden opportunity to fulfill that wish. And I could continue being a stay-at-home mom." She glanced out the side window at her house. "There's a huge part of me that wants to say yes."

"And there's a small part of you saying no?"

"Not really. But I have to think of Rafe. It's been just the two of us for a couple of years now and I don't want him to feel neglected. Having a newborn is very time-consuming, as you know."

She noticed a subtle change in his facial expression and his eyes clouded over ever so slightly. "I'm sorry, Prescott. I shouldn't have said that. It was insensitive and stupid."

"No, I didn't take it that way. You're not the type of person to purposely be mean, Annie." His eyebrows rose a bit. "But it is what it is. Every day that passes... it's hard to believe I'll never see them again. Like a chunk of my heart is missing that can only be filled by their presence." He shook his head. "And the months roll by. And no one can find them."

"Maybe the private investigator will come up with some leads. You never know."

He smiled. "I do believe in miracles."

She opened the door and jumped out. "I'll see you later," she said and waved as he pulled away from the curb.

When she got inside, she went straight to her MacBook and wrote an e-mail to her lawyer in San Francisco. She wanted to ask him if he could give her the name of an attorney in the area who handled adoptions.

Just in case.

* * * *

Rafe would be eleven-years-old on October twenty-first. She snagged him as he ran out the door to play on the swings in the back yard. "What do you want to do for your big day this Saturday?"

He stopped mid-stride. "Ummm. Can I have my friends over?"

"Sure. What do you want to eat at your party?"

He rolled his eyes. "Hot dogs, potato chips, Coke, a chocolate birthday cake. Oh, and lots of presents."

Annie laughed. "You ask for the exact same thing every year, Rafe. Do you ever think of breaking out of the mold? I could barbecue chicken, make potato salad."

"I love hot dogs, potato chips and Coke, Mom."

"Then what do you want for your birthday present?"

"You know what I want but you told me it's too expensive," he said and rushed out the back door.

She sighed, staring at his back as he ran down the stairs. Cameron and Annie had given him a Nintendo DS years ago. She planned on buying him a Sony PlayStation, quite an upgrade from the Nintendo DS. He'd be completely surprised.

She sent an E-vite to five of his friends, and then asked him if he wanted to invite any grownups.

"I know you want to invite Prescott, Mom," he said. "But do you think he'll want to come to a kid's birthday party?"

Wow. She sure didn't want to get into a discussion with him about her relationship with Prescott. "I'll ask him."

Later that day Prescott was unloading supplies from the back of his truck, and Annie approached him tentatively. "Rafe wanted," she began, rethought. "Rafe and I want to know if you'd like to come to his birthday party this Saturday."

He broke out in a wide grin. "I'd love to." He glanced at the ground for a moment and, she swore, when his gaze met hers, tears rimmed his eyes. "I never got to be with Dylan for any of his birthdays."

"He wants you to be there, Prescott," Annie said and ducked her head. "And so do I."

He reached out and lifted her chin with his fingers. "Then I'll be there."

She turned and walked back into the house. Every time she was around him lately her heart bumped up and down and it almost felt as if she were hyperventilating.

What was happening to her?

Saturday arrived crisp and clear, in the low sixties. It was a perfect day for six high-energy boys to race around the back yard, shoot basketball, gobble down all the food as if none of them had eaten all day, then return for huge slices of Annie's homemade chocolate fudge cake.

When it came time to open his gifts, Rafe couldn't wait to tear off the wrappings. And the look on his face was priceless when he realized she'd given him something as rad as a Sony Play Station 3.

The boys were about to hook up the PS3, when Prescott interrupted them. "Hey, Rafe. Did you think I'd come to your birthday bash and not give you a present?"

Rafe shrugged. "I dunno. You're not my age or anything. I just wanted Mom to have a friend to hang around with."

Prescott pointed outside. "It's in the back of my truck."

Rafe smiled and ran toward the front door, swung it wide, and then raced down the front pathway, through the pergola, out to the truck. He grabbed the tail gate, swung it open and let out a loud whoop, something Annie hadn't heard in a long time.

"A bike," he yelled and glanced toward the porch where she stood next to Prescott.

Prescott strode down the stairs, pulled the bike from the truck and placed it on the ground. Rafe jumped on, grabbed the handlebars and squeezed the brake handles. "Eighteen speeds?"

"Yup." Prescott grinned back at him.

"I love it," Rafe shouted. "Thank you."

Rafe took a quick ride, pedaling along the paths through the yard, down the driveway, and then down the street and back again with a smile on his face the entire time.

It had been a great day. Over two years had passed since Cam's death, and this was a whole new environment, new friends, new home. And Rafe was allowing another man into his life.

CHAPTER FIFTEEN

Halloween marked the beginning of the season's festivities. Rafe and Annie would be celebrating Thanksgiving and Christmas in their new home, surrounded by new friends, and the birth of Allessandra's baby was just around the corner.

Prescott joined Annie and Rafe when they went trick-or-treating. He enjoyed seeing Rafe knock on neighbors' doors, yelling "Trick or Treat."

When they returned home, Rafe, exhausted and happy, dumped his pillow case filled with candy onto the front room floor. Prescott and Annie laughed at the expression on his face as he dug through his loot. After he separated the chocolate pieces from the bubble gum and cookies, he dragged himself upstairs to bed and Annie tucked him in.

She tiptoed down the stairs. Prescott was sitting on the couch in the dark. The only light came from the candles they'd stuck inside the pumpkins sitting on the windowsills.

She slumped down on the couch a few feet away from him, leaned her head back, and let out a big sigh. "That was exhausting."

He put his arm around her shoulders and pulled her to his chest. His gaze roved toward her mouth. He bent his head and placed his lips softly over hers, pulled back and held her gaze for a few seconds before he dipped his head again. He widened the kiss to a sensual dance of tongues, slid his arm off her shoulders and leaned his head back on the couch.

"What's wrong?" she whispered.

He shook his head and stared at the ceiling. "I don't want to push you."

Annie grinned. "Don't apologize. I enjoyed it."

He turned to face her, eyebrows drawn downward. "There hasn't been anyone since Patti. It never felt right. Like I'd be betraying her, or something." He leaned forward, placed his elbows on his knees and cradled his head with both hands. "If she took Dylan, there's nothing wrong with my kissing you. But if they were kidnapped... " He turned his face in her direction. "Annie, I can't live my life waiting for them to be found."

He raked his fingers through his hair. "And every time I talk to the cops or the feds all they tell me is, "I'm sorry, Mr. Beemiller. We haven't found any clues to their whereabouts." It's so damn frustrating."

"How's it going with your attorney?"

"I talked with him the other day. The hardest part is that his P.I. has to search, and I quote, "any place that Patti might go." He has to show that his private investigator has done everything possible to find her." He let out a deep breath. "Am I doing the right thing, divorcing her now?"

She knelt down in front of him and placed a hand on each side of his face, stared into his big hazel eyes. "Do you still love her?"

"She was my first love. There will always be a place in my heart for her. But if she took my son, a part of me hates her. When I'm with you, I forget all about her. And when I kissed you... Hell, I don't regret that."

"Pres, regret and guilt are two emotions that'll eat you up. Only you can decide what you should do with your life right now." She tapped her finger on his chest. "If it feels right in your heart, do it and don't look back."

He stood, reached out his hand, and helped her up. "I have to get up early tomorrow."

They walked to the foyer and he wrapped his arms around her waist.

"Allessandra asked me if I could find the name of an attorney who handles adoptions," he said. "She's assuming you don't want to tell her no to her face because you think she'll be mad at you."

Annie smiled up at him. "I have the name of an adoption attorney in Sea Cliff."

His eyebrows flew upward. "Really?"

"I want to talk to Rafe again. I really like Allessandra and respect her for being so unselfish. She's thinking about what's best for her unborn child. She knows she's not ready to be a mom. She could have gone the easy route and had an abortion but she chose not to. That's admirable."

"So you're doing this for her?"

"No, of course not. I want to do this for me and Rafe." She paused. "I want another child... and a brother or sister for Rafe. At times I feel as if this opportunity has fallen into my life for a reason and I want to pick it up and run with it."

His mouth curved up at the edges.

"What?" she said. "You look like the cat who ate the canary."

"You said you want to do this. So you've made a decision."

She grinned. "I guess you're right. I've made up my mind but I have to talk to Rafe again to make sure he wants this, too."

He kissed her one more time, opened the front door, and walked down the steps. He turned around when he reached the bottom of the stairs. "If you decide to do it, I'd love to be around to watch that little kid grow up."

She smiled, waved, and shut the door.

How would this end up?

* * * *

A few days after Halloween, Rafe stayed home from school with a cough and a low-grade fever. While playing checkers, she said, "Thanksgiving's almost here. Is there anyone special you'd like to invite?"

He jumped her checker and grinned. "Allessandra?"

She crowned his checker. "Anyone else?"

He jumped her again and smiled. "Prescott?"

She held back a smile of her own and jumped one of his kings. "Prescott, huh?"

He stopped playing, a funny expression on his face. "Are you guys in love?"

Annie sat back in her chair and gave him a stern look. "What makes you say that?"

A playful smile crept over his lips. "I see the way he looks at you. The same way Daddy used to."

Annie's insides lurched, remembering Cam with a pang in her heart for the first time in months. "I'll always love your father, Rafe. You know that, right?"

He nodded, but still didn't return to the checker game. "Is it okay to marry two times?"

She could see where this conversation was headed and wasn't prepared to answer. She should have anticipated the questions would come up one day. She just didn't think it would be today.

"Yes, it's legal to marry two times. In fact, people get divorced and remarry more than twice. Some get remarried three, four, or more times during their lifetime. But your daddy and I didn't get divorced. We loved each other very much." She paused. "I'd like to get married again someday, Rafe, but it'll have to be someone very, very special 'cause your daddy was one of a kind."

He nodded, reached out, and moved one of his checkers. "You told me once that Prescott was a special person. Does that mean you guys are gonna get married?"

She suppressed a laugh. "Umm, no, we're not getting married. We aren't even dating, Honey. But if we do start dating, you'll be the first to know."

"So, can he come to Thanksgiving? And Allessandra, too?"

"I'll call Allessandra. And I'll ask Prescott next time I see him. I think we should invite Barb and Stacey as well."

That afternoon, while Rafe was taking a nap, Annie walked around the house, searching for Prescott. "Hello? Are you back here?"

"Over here," he yelled and rounded the corner. "Is something wrong? You didn't take Rafe to school today."

"He's got a little cold. We're spending some quality time together, playing checkers and crazy eights."

"Sounds fun. The sort of thing I'd like to do with my son," he said, his lips set in a tight line. "That's what makes me so angry, all those experiences stolen from me."

Annie laid a hand on his arm, stared into his eyes. "Rafe and I would like you to join us for Thanksgiving dinner."

His lips turned up in a smile. "I'd love to. What can I bring? I make a killer turkey."

"Great. Rafe will be so happy. I think you've really captured that little guy's heart." Annie paused. Oh, what the hell. "In fact, his heart's not the only one you've captured." Her face burned and she tried to appear nonchalant.

His expression turned serious again. "Would you like to go out sometime? I want to get to know you better. We could go to dinner, just the two of us, no distractions."

"I'd like that. How about tomorrow night?" His smile could have lit up a stadium. "If Rafe's better, I'll ask Abby if she could babysit."

"It's a plan." The grin on his face stretched from ear to ear.

CHAPTER SIXTEEN

The following morning Rafe felt fine, and Annie told Prescott they were on for that evening. They could drop Rafe off at Abby's at six o'clock.

When the hour approached for their date, Annie put on a short black dress and high heels. Her weight had held steady since high school at one hundred and twenty pounds and the material clung to her figure like a second skin. Her hair had grown just past her shoulders, and her bangs swayed a little above her lashes. She applied a bit of eye liner, mascara, and a dash of pink lipstick and was ready to go. A few minutes after spraying on her favorite perfume, the doorbell rang and she rushed downstairs to answer it.

And there he stood, wearing a dark blue suit, white shirt, and maroon tie, his hair neatly cut and his mustache trimmed. But his goatee was missing. And it had covered a very sexy cleft in his chin. The scent of his cologne wafted through the screen door. He smelled delicious.

"Annie," he whispered. "You're beautiful. I feel like a teenager with a crush. As your son would say, you look totally rad."

She blushed. Cam had always told her she was beautiful but that felt like light years ago. And she hadn't dressed up for anything or anyone since Cam's funeral.

"Thank you. You look handsome as well."

Rafe joined them in the foyer. "Wow. You look totally rad, Mom. Where're you going?"

Prescott and Annie glanced at each other and laughed. Prescott reached for Annie's elbow to escort her out the door.

"What's so funny, you guys?" Rafe asked, frowning.

Prescott mussed the top of Rafe's hair. "That's what I told your mom, too, Rafe. That she looked totally rad tonight. I'm taking her to a fancy restaurant."

Rafe nodded and ran out to the truck. They dropped him off at Abby's then headed east on Main Street.

"There's a small town on Route A33 with one of the best restaurants in the area. Villa Montalvo. People come from as far away as Los Angeles to eat there. I was able to make reservations since it's the middle of the week."

"I'm just happy to be out of the house," she said, feeling like a little kid. "I've been stuck inside since the weather turned cold and I swear I'm talking to myself more and more when I'm alone. Scary, huh?"

His laugh, deep and sexy, reminded her again of how good it felt to be around him, a male adult, a good-looking male adult, a good-looking male adult who had feelings for her. Did she say scary? Her insides felt like Jell-O. She hadn't been on a date in years.

"You're just not used to being away from the coast, Annie. It's not that cold here. It dipped down to fifty-five degrees last night."

She laughed. "You're right. I'm just a spoiled brat. Sausalito's weather is pretty darn mild, but it can get to the low forties during the night there in the winter, you know."

"I've been to San Francisco a couple of times during my college years. What I didn't like was the wind. I walked across the Golden Gate Bridge and the gusts were blowing up to forty miles per hour."

"Makes you appreciate the mild breezes in Brandiss, huh?"

Their conversation and the easy drive relaxed Annie's jangled nerves. The only thing between Brandiss and Villa Montalvo were green rolling hills and lots of cows. The restaurant, located in an old Victorian house, had a small white sign indicating it had been in business since 1952, a family-run establishment.

A curved driveway led up to the front where a valet opened the door and helped Annie out of the car. They walked up the steps leading to beveled glass doors, through them to the foyer. A concierge escorted them to the back of a dining room lined with windows overlooking a large yard. Two weeping willows dotted the back garden and a pathway led to a bridge curved over a small pond.

A white linen tablecloth covered their table, set with gleaming silverware and a red rose in a crystal vase. The concierge handed them menus. He asked if they wanted a beverage, after which he left them discreetly alone.

"This is lovely, Prescott. How did you find it?"

"People in Brandiss are frequent patrons. I've always wanted to eat here but never had anyone to share it with. Until now."

A warm blush crept along her cheeks and she ducked her head. "I'm flattered."

"My pleasure." He fingered the tiny rose inside the vase. "You know, we don't ever get to spend much time alone."

"Life gets in the way. But I run into you while you're working sometimes," she teased.

He nodded. "Or when I'm taking a break with Allessandra."

Annie laughed. "We were all alone that time you made me dinner at your house, remember?"

"Anything you want to know about me, Annie, feel free to ask." He reached inside the breast pocket of his suit jacket. "I happen to have an application I downloaded from E-Harmony dot com. We should each fill one out."

Annie stared, wide-eyed as he pulled out the ticket from the parking valet. She gave him a withering look and he chuckled.

She couldn't suppress a laugh and shook her head. "Oh, you are so bad."

He looked across the table at her, a serious expression on his face. "As I said before, I'm an open book, Annie."

She arranged the napkin on her lap. "Tell me how you met your wife, unless that makes you uncomfortable."

"No, I'd be happy to tell you." He leaned back in his chair. "I was studying for my B.A. in Structural Engineering at UC Santa Barbara. I had to get my prerequisites out of the way, so I took an English Lit class and there she was."

"Love at first sight?"

"Yeah. My first love. She was so different from me: unstructured, a real hippy. Sounds politically incorrect but it's the truth. And me? I knew exactly what I was going to do—get married, have two point five kids, live here in California. I had everything all planned out."

"The age-old opposites attract thing?"

"I guess you could say that. We were together our last two years at UC, but it was a pretty volatile relationship. We broke up every few months. We'd make up and everything would be great for a while, then we'd have another fight.

"After graduation, we moved in together, more out of convenience than anything else. Then she got pregnant. I talked her into marrying me before she had the baby. Thought it was the right thing to do."

"What did she want to do?"

"Have an abortion. But I said it wasn't fair because I did want the child. I said I'd stay home, take care of the baby. She could work if she wanted to. But as it turned out, I got a job in Santa Barbara that paid well with good hours. So I bought a house in Carpinteria, turned one of the bedrooms into a studio for her so she could paint. She had Dylan. Nine months later, she and Dylan were gone.

"I get a call every few months from the FBI, telling me someone saw them here or there. But it's never them. I'm learning to let go, trying to move on."

"What was it like coming back to Brandiss, after what happened?"

"I hadn't been away that long. But when I returned, I have to admit I felt kinda funny."

She looked at him quizzically.

He shrugged. "You know, the whole thing about the spouse being the prime suspect. But no one in Brandiss believed I had anything to do with Patti and Dylan's disappearance. They could have shunned me, but they took me in, supported me. And when I started looking for work, everyone in town tried to help me out. They could have done a lot of the work themselves but they hired me instead. They believed in me."

"And you made it," Annie said. "You have your own business. You got on with your life. You have a lot to be proud of, Prescott."

"I never took another drink. I put my nose to the grindstone and worked my butt off. Not just for me, though. I did it for all the people who believed in me, who had faith in me when I had very little of it myself."

He paused, stared out the window a moment. "You know, it wasn't just the fact I told everyone I wasn't involved in their disappearance, or that the police and FBI didn't have any evidence to pin it on me. They're actually going to put the story on *America's Most Wanted*. John Walsh takes a personal interest in stories involving young kids, because of what happened to his own son. I talked to one of the AMW people months ago and they're still working on fitting me into their schedule."

"Whenever your name comes up in conversation, no one's ever said anything negative about you. All I hear are complements about your work ethic, your personality, how honest you are. And everybody says how sorry they are about what happened to you in Santa Barbara."

"What about you, Annie?" He reached across the table and took her hand. "Tell me something about yourself that I don't already know."

His warm hand holding hers made her feel less embarrassed, gave her the strength to tell her own story to someone other than the grief counselor she'd seen in Sausalito.

"Well, you know I was married to Cameron. He died about two years ago. And we had one child—Rafe." She covered her face with her hand. "God, I'm not doing a very good job of this. I sound like a robot."

He gently pulled her hand from her face and smiled. "It's me you're talking to, Annie. And I want to know everything about you. Whether you think it's boring or silly, I don't care. I want to know what's behind that beautiful façade."

She took a deep breath and let it out slowly. "Cam and I had a good marriage. We were very happy. I didn't go back to work after Rafe was born. Davidson Construction, Cam's business, was doing extremely well."

"Sounds like you had a nice little family."

"Yeah. It was just Cam and Rafe and me. My mom and dad both passed away a few years before Rafe was born."

"And Cameron's parents?"

"They passed away before he and I got married. Anyway, after my parents died, I took some of my inheritance and bought Cam the truck he always wanted." She grinned, recalling Cam's enthusiastic response when he found it parked in their driveway. "He always said he'd rather use the profits from Davidson Construction for employee raises and bonuses. He refused to squander money on a luxury vehicle."

"Sounds like a good guy."

She nodded. "Yes, he was." She paused, emotions welling inside her heart. "Anyway, I could spend my inheritance however I wanted, and I was determined to give him something he deserved. He'd put so much of his time and heart into the business. It was my way of saying thank you for giving up so much."

As she felt the rush of past feelings, tears rimmed her eyes, and slowly escaped down her cheeks. "He was driving to Home Depot when an eighteen-wheeler, going way over the speed limit, broadsided his truck. He had extensive brain damage, massive internal injuries. He was in a coma. He only lived for a few hours after the accident." She let out a sigh of relief. "You know, I haven't told that story to anyone in years."

He leaned across the table and gently wiped away her tears with his fingers. "That must have hit you hard. Everything changed in an instant."

"It was awful. I didn't think I'd ever feel anything for anyone again until... "

Silence permeated the air between them.

"Annie?" he whispered.

"I do have feelings for you, Prescott, but I'm scared. You've had a shocking thing happen in your life. Patti and Dylan are still missing."

"Annie, if she left me, I don't owe her a damn thing. And I know the statistics when someone goes missing. I can't wait forever." He inhaled deeply. "So, would you like some dessert?"

After triple-fudge brownies with vanilla ice cream, they drove home. On the way they listened to their favorite *Gladiator* CD. They picked up Rafe, and then Prescott dropped them off at the house. That night Annie had another dream. But this one was different from the others.

CHAPTER SEVENTEEN

Annie walks down the aisle of a church. Not the church where Cameron and she were married, but the church in Santa Barbara where she sometimes accompanied her parents when they came to visit. She hadn't been going to church regularly since starting university, but that was more of a time thing than anything else. And it made her Mom and Dad happy if she attended Mass, so she'd go with them.

Every time she entered a church, she got goose bumps. The light filtering through the stained glass windows, the camaraderie when everyone's singing along, the congregation's responses to the priest made her heart soar.

Her dad was still alive. She held onto his arm and they did "the walk" down the aisle. The wedding march was playing. The pews were filled with people, their faces indistinguishable, blurred. When they arrived at the steps leading to the altar, they turned toward each other and her father lifted her black veil.

Annie smiled and he smiled back. He kissed her on her left, and then her right cheek, and said, "I love you, Annie. And I love the big guy, too."

She chuckled. "I love you, too, Dad. And so does he."

She gathered up her dress. It was made of black lace—a beautiful gown with black pearls intricately sewn along the bodice. She turned her head toward the back of the church. The train of the dress trailed down the middle aisle, through the front doors, and slipped down the front steps as far as she could see.

She stepped up to the altar, and a man in a black tuxedo walked toward her, his face blurred, just like you see on television when they don't want the public to see who they're filming. She didn't know who he was.

He took her hand and guided her toward him. When she glanced down to gather the side of her dress, he whispered, "Hi, Annie."

It was Prescott.

She looked up in surprise, but he disappeared. She turned around. The pews were empty. There was no one in the church. The music stopped, her dad was gone, the groom disappeared. She suddenly felt chilled. When she looked down she realized she didn't have a stitch of clothing on. She crossed her arms over her chest, started to flee, and noticed there was a rocking chair next to her—the same rocking chair that was next to her bed in their house in Brandiss. She sat down and woke up with a start.

It was five-forty-five a.m., so Annie got up and took a shower. Perhaps it would de-clutter her brain. She still felt confused, a bit disoriented. With the shower turned to as strong a flow as possible, she tried to make sense out of her dream.

Could the black wedding gown have a negative meaning? But at the end she was no longer wearing it. Her dad said he loved the big guy but Cameron wasn't a big man. On the other hand, Prescott was about six-foot-three and weighed over two hundred pounds. Was her dad speaking to her from the grave, giving her a thumbs up with regard to Prescott?

Annie slowly stepped out of the shower. Had she gotten any of it right?

* * * *

Allessandra, Stacey, Barb, and Prescott accepted Annie's invitation to join them for Thanksgiving dinner. Rafe loved having company, the more the merrier. His grandparents were dead. Annie's sister Kathy lived in Southern California with her daughters and grandkids, and Annie didn't see her often. Rafe enjoyed it when people visited.

Thanksgiving morning, Rafe walked past Annie's bedroom doorway and she patted the comforter. "Morning, Honey. Come and sit here."

He smiled, his hair mussed from sleep, and rubbed his eyes. "Morning, Mom," he said and kissed her on the cheek.

"Sleep well?"

"Mm—hmm," he mumbled, snuggled next to her and closed his eyes.

"Have you thought about what you and I talked about? You know, how Allessandra wants us to adopt her baby?"

He opened his eyes wide. "Yeah."

"And what do you think about it?"

"What do you wanna do?"

"I haven't worked outside the home since you were born. I definitely have the time to devote to taking care of a baby. Plus I have lots of space in my heart to love another child."

"Most of my friends at school have brothers and sisters."

"Would you like that, too?"

"I don't know. I guess so."

"Do you think we should tell Allessandra we'd like to be her baby's new mommy and big brother?"

His eyes focused on somewhere to the side of Annie, staring. "I think so." He bolted upright and clapped his hands. "Can I tell her?"

"Well, she'll be here today, so it would be the perfect time."

He smiled. "Okay." He hugged her, jumped off the bed and ran down the stairs.

Prescott arrived early to prepare the turkey. Rafe answered the door, and Annie heard them exchanging bits of information about the Macy's Thanksgiving Day Parade, showing all morning on the television. Rafe always waited with anticipation for the Spongebob Squarepants balloon to soar between the office buildings of Manhattan.

Annie stood at the kitchen sink and the heavy tread of Prescott's boots crossed the linoleum floor. She turned to greet him and collided with the hard muscles of his chest.

"Wow, you scared me." She didn't finish her sentence before he covered her mouth in a kiss.

"Happy Thanksgiving, Annie." He wrapped his arms around her waist and gently pushed her up against the back of the countertop. Their gazes locked and she could feel his arousal.

She draped her arms around his neck, pulled his head down and kissed him softly, gliding her tongue under his mustache along his smooth lips. Her body tingled. It was only a kiss, but she was already finding it hard to catch her breath.

Prescott's breathing quickened, his chest expanded and contracted against her breasts. Their lips met again, their tongues entwined. He tasted like coffee and cream, the scent of his cologne all male, everything about him intoxicating.

Annie glided her hands slowly down his back, grasped him below the waist and moved her pelvis slowly from side to side, enticed by the bulge beneath his zipper.

He pulled away sharply, and her hands fell to her sides. He backed away from her embrace. "I don't know what I was thinking," he said, his breathing labored. "Rafe's in the other room."

She reached out for him and brought him back into her arms, laid her head on his chest and sighed. "No one's made me feel like a woman in a long time, Prescott."

He placed his hand under her chin, tipped her head back and grinned mischievously. "I'm happy to oblige you any time."

A rush of heat traveled from her neck to her forehead. "And I'll take you up on your offer sooner than you think."

He bent down for another kiss just as Rafe popped his head into the kitchen.

"Mom, when's... ."

Rafe's smile warmed her heart. "You want to know when dinner will be served?"

Prescott turned toward him. "It's quite a ways off, buddy. Would you like to help me get this bird in the oven?"

Rafe ran the rest of the way into the kitchen and washed his hands. The three of them worked together, listening to Vivaldi's Four Seasons, the *Gladiator* soundtrack, and other CDs in Annie's collection. She and Prescott had similar musical tastes which Annie found refreshing. Cam and she could never agree on what music to play at home or in the car.

Allessandra, Stacey, and Barb arrived later. They all sat in the front room and talked about people in Brandiss, Allessandra's ever-growing belly, Barb's travel plans with her boyfriend. There wasn't a moment of silence, like sharing a holiday with relatives.

When it came time to sit down to dinner, Annie took a chair at the head of the table, Rafe sat to her left next to Stacey with Barb at the other end, and Prescott took a chair between Annie and Allessandra.

They filled their plates before everyone looked around the table at each other.

"Rafe, would you like to make a toast?" Annie winked at him.

He picked up his wine glass filled with sparkling cider. "Mom and I want to make a toast to Allessandra," he said and looked at Allessandra across the table.

Allessandra smiled and raised her glass.

"We want to adopt your baby," he announced with a grin.

Allessandra slowly placed her wine glass back on the table. She turned to Annie, and then looked back at Rafe. A solitary tear escaped down her cheek. "Are you guys for real?"

Annie nodded and raised her glass in Allessandra's direction. "If you'd still like us to be your baby's new family, both Rafe and I accept your invitation."

"Thank you," Allessandra whispered.

"That is so cool," Stacey said, clinking her glass with Rafe's.

"Congratulations." Barb tipped her glass in Annie's direction and smiled.

Prescott clinked his glass against Rafe's, and then Annie's and grinned. "That's exciting news, you two."

Allessandra picked up her glass again. "That is awesome."

"I have the name of an attorney who handles adoptions, unless you already have one picked out," Annie said.

"No, I was waiting for... No, I don't have one. Can you set up a meeting?"

"I'll call him tomorrow."

The rest of dinner was relaxed and everyone enjoyed themselves. At Rafe's bedtime, Prescott volunteered to tuck him in. They forced Allessandra to stay off her feet while the rest of them cleaned up. At ten o'clock they were exhausted and Barb, Stacey, and Allessandra headed home.

After Allessandra hugged Annie and whispered "thank you," Annie closed the front door and turned toward Prescott. "Would you like to stay a while?"

He smiled.

"I just want to check on Rafe first." Annie held up her index finger. "I'll be right back."

She walked up the stairs, thinking about the day. It had been the nearest thing to a typical family Thanksgiving since Cam's death. Annie was so glad Rafe had the opportunity to enjoy the holiday with this group of people, that it didn't turn out to be another day with only Annie and Rafe sitting across the table from each another.

Rafe was sleeping, snoring lightly. Annie made sure he hadn't kicked off his comforter, and returned to the front room. The candles still flickered, but the lamps were turned off. Prescott sat on the couch, in the same place as the night of their first kiss.

After Annie sat down, Prescott put his arm around her shoulders and she leaned toward him and placed her head on his chest. His heart beat against her ear and she sighed. He threaded his fingers through her hair.

Annie wound her arms around his neck, weaved her hands through the thick hair above his shirt collar toward the crown of his head. He dipped his head, touched his lips to hers and their tongues danced a slow, weaving waltz.

He pulled his mouth away and dropped kisses on her eyelids, cheeks, down her neck. She leaned back, allowing him the fullness of her breasts. His hand glided down the front of her shirt, brushing over her hardened nipple. He moaned her name as he brought his mouth down to cover the protruding nub between his teeth and sucked gently through the thin cloth. A low whimper escaped her gritted teeth.

Annie trailed her hand toward the zipper of his jeans and gently caressed him. His groaning escalated, his kisses more urgent and forceful. He gently slid the shirt down her shoulders and leaned away.

"You're a beautiful woman, Annie. I want to make love to you."

A raspy whisper escaped her lips. "I want you." She drew in a deep breath and exhaled. "Now."

She unzipped his jeans, gently pulled him outside his briefs, held him in both her hands and moved her fingers slowly up and down his swollen length. He unzipped her skirt and brought it down past her feet. His eyes widened at the sight of her thigh-high nylons and black thong.

"Do you have... ?" she started to say.

He reached into his back pocket, pulled out his wallet and extracted a small gold packet.

Annie smiled and pulled his jeans down.

He kicked off his shoes and pants, slipped his shirt off over his head. Annie threw off her own shirt. He removed her panties, and she took him in her hands. He ripped the packet open and extracted the condom.

Taking the bright gold circle of rubber, Annie smiled while she rolled it onto him before guiding him between her legs. He moved slowly, then more avidly, both tender and passionate.

She savored the waves of her orgasm, one after the other, followed by Prescott's pulsing throbs.

They lay silent, grasping each other, their breathing hard and fast.

"I love you, Annie," he whispered. "And you don't have to say anything."

Annie tried to focus, her mind reeling from the sexual high. "I love you, too." She let out a pent-up breath. "It's a relief to finally say the words."

They snuggled and watched the fluttering flames in the fireplace slowly disappear. Morning would come soon. She walked him to the door, and they kissed goodbye.

This Thanksgiving would linger in her mind forever.

Nothing could compare to the thrill of falling in love.

CHAPTER EIGHTEEN

The next day Annie made an appointment to see Mr. Mayer and then drove with Allessandra to Sea Cliff to meet him. A distinguished looking man in his mid-fifties, he was dressed in a grey pin-striped suit, white shirt, dark tie, loafers and a Rolex watch. He impressed Annie with his extensive knowledge of adoption law and explained the legalities, time frame, and necessary paperwork.

He answered all their questions and gave them the papers they needed to fill out. He said he'd try to schedule a home review within the next few months. Timing was crucial, given Allessandra's due date of March seventeenth and the fact she'd just been in the hospital, and a premature birth concerned them.

They were walking across the parking lot to Annie's car when Annie said, "I have to ask you something."

They reached the Mercedes, and Annie looked at Allessandra over the hood. "Did our meeting make you more or less sure about wanting me to adopt your baby?"

Allessandra took a deep breath, letting it out on a sigh. "I feel better now, for sure. Saying I wanted this for my baby wasn't a reality until I actually did something about it." She opened the car door and settled into the seat as Annie started the car. "I've done what I said I would do. It's real now."

Annie smiled. "I'm glad. You still up for lunch?"

"Can we skip it?"

Annie glanced over at her. "You okay?"

Allessandra turned her head toward the car window. "Sure. I just don't have much of an appetite."

They reached the house and both changed clothes. Annie went into the backyard and picked weeds and watered the plants but she insisted Allessandra rest first, especially after the holiday and their meeting with Mr. Mayer.

Prescott had been working along the back side of the house and they all took a short break in the afternoon. They sipped iced tea and Allessandra smiled. "So are you two guys an item or what? Is my baby gonna have a daddy too?"

A piece of chipped ice lodged itself in Annie's throat and she choked. Prescott patted her on the back until she caught her breath.

"What makes you think that?" Annie said, still sputtering.

"I saw both of you when you came to visit me in the hospital. You were holding hands." She grinned like a young kid with a secret.

Prescott sat a little straighter in his chair and cleared his throat. "We've gone out on one date." He glanced at Annie and smiled.

Allessandra pumped her fist in the air. "Yes!"

Annie shook her head in mock disgust and Prescott laughed. Annie gave them both a stern look. "May I remind you that you're both my employees and break time is over."

Prescott and Allessandra stood in unison, glanced at each other, marched out the back door and down the stairs.

"Take it easy, Allessandra," Annie shouted.

Annie was left sitting alone in the kitchen with a big grin on her face, thinking how lucky she was to have the two of them in her life.

* * * *

Christmas was fast approaching. Everything in Annie's life was happening so fast. Allessandra had been in the hospital, Rafe celebrated his eleventh birthday, then Halloween and Thanksgiving. They told Allessandra they wanted to adopt her baby, followed by the night with Prescott.

Allessandra had been spotting on and off for weeks, even though she was resting as the doctor ordered. Annie forbade her to help in the garden for more than an hour on the days she was available, and only allowed her to pull weeds if she sat on a soft cushion, no bending over or straining. Annie certainly didn't want to be the cause of a miscarriage.

The days were getting shorter. Each evening Annie helped Rafe with his homework, and they'd take turns reading to each other. They watched a little television then he was off to bed by nine o'clock.

Annie hadn't seen Prescott much since Thanksgiving. He'd

signed up for a state-required two-week course in Structural Engineering at Santa Barbara City College, a bit of a drive for him each night. The class hours were seven p.m. to ten p.m., Monday through Friday.

They talked on the phone every evening while he drove to class and shared their day's activities. He worked a side job during the day in Carpinteria, south of Santa Barbara, which allowed him to jet from the job site to class in no time at all.

She'd been anxiously awaiting the completion of the baby's room; however, it was taking more time than originally expected due to Prescott's classes and side job. His schedule wouldn't return to normal until Christmas. Then they could see each other again on a regular basis.

Annie spent time sewing curtains and buying furniture for the nursery to make it cozy and inviting for the baby's arrival. She wanted it to look perfect. Winter had set in, and the garden needed only light tending. She planned to wait until spring to plant a new crop of vegetables. She watered the flowers each day, which forced her outside to smell the fresh air, the sun's gentle rays striking the paleness from her face.

The days fairly flew by. Rafe remained in school until Christmas vacation began on December twenty-first and Annie planned to do most of her Christmas shopping online. Driving to Santa Barbara and shopping at the mall by herself wasn't as exciting as in the past when she lived in Sausalito. Back then she and Cam spent hours in San Francisco, fighting the crowds. Yet they enjoyed their time together, ending the day with dinner at a nice restaurant.

Allessandra hadn't called Annie in several days. She was taking finals at school and resting. March was right around the corner and Allessandra had about three months before she was due to have her baby.

Rafe hounded Annie every day and pleaded with her to take him to the mall so he could make up his Christmas list. When Prescott dropped by one day, Rafe asked Annie again.

Prescott spoke up before Annie could answer. "I could take you to the mall in Santa Barbara if you want. We could all three go and make a day of it. Have lunch while we're there and do a little Christmas shopping. If your mom says it's okay."

"What do you think, Rafe?" Annie asked, smiling.

Rafe hopped up and down with nervous energy. "Can we go today?"

"It's up to your mom," Prescott said.

The two of them turned in Annie's direction, their eyebrows raised in question.

"I'd enjoy that," she said.

Rafe grabbed his coat, ran out the door and reached the truck before she had a chance to put on her jacket.

They spent the rest of the day in the small shops of Santa Barbara on State Street as well as the newly-renovated mall in the center of the city where Santa Claus was visiting. They had dinner at the Penca Azul, a Mexican restaurant Prescott frequented during his college days. They ended the day with Italian gelato at eight o'clock.

Later that evening, Prescott's truck pulled up in the driveway and they turned around to see Rafe sound asleep in the back seat. Prescott walked up the front steps, holding Rafe in his arms. Once inside Prescott tucked him into bed, and then he and Annie retired to the kitchen.

He plopped down in the kitchen chair. "How do you do it? I never knew such a small human could have that much physical stamina." He leaned back in his chair and blew out a big puff of air.

"I know, I know," Annie laughed. "He's a ball of energy at eleven."

He shook his head and grinned. "He's a great kid, Annie. You and Cameron did a fine job raising him. He's polite, respectful, doesn't use bad language. I'd be thrilled to have a son like him." All of a sudden it was as if a curtain had been pulled down over his face, the smile wiped clean from his lips.

"You missed out on so much with Dylan. And I know Rafe is no substitute... "

"No, don't say that, Annie. It breaks my heart that my son's gone but sharing the holidays with you and Rafe helps make up for the loss."

"You're planning to spend Christmas with us, right?" she asked. "Rafe will want to show you what he got, plus I bought you something. I want to give it to you in person."

"I wouldn't miss it. I have something for both of you as well."

Just as they finished their coffee Rafe stumbled into the kitchen, rubbing his eyes. "I'm thirsty, Mom. Can I have a glass of water?"

Prescott and Annie knew that a quiet, uninterrupted evening was wishful thinking. They turned toward each other and smiled. Any opportunity for intimacy wasn't going to happen tonight.

Thanksgiving had been the first and only time they'd made love. There hadn't been one single opportunity since. Between having Rafe at home, Christmas gifts to buy, and Prescott's busy schedule, the stars weren't aligning to enhance its happening in the near future, either.

CHAPTER NINETEEN

Christmas day arrived with freezing temperatures and the wind blew so hard the tree branches brushed against the sides of the house.

Rafe kissed Annie on the cheek. "Merry Christmas, Mom."

She opened one eye half-way. "Aw, Rafe, can't you let me sleep in?" she mumbled and snuggled further underneath the down comforter.

He bounced up and down on the king-size bed as if it was a trampoline. "I... want... to... open... presents," his voice wavered with each bounce.

She dragged herself out from under the warm comforter, and they walked down the stairs. After Rafe rooted through his stocking that hung from the fireplace mantel, he searched around under the tree and found the boxes labeled with his name, grabbed them, and brought the gifts over to the couch.

He tore the wrapping off the biggest one and his face broke out in an enormous smile. "How did you know?"

"I always know," she teased.

He squinted. "Prescott told you, didn't he? After we came back from the mall."

She furrowed her eyebrows in mock confusion. "I don't know what you're talking about."

"I never told you I wanted Guitar Hero, Mom."

"Then you should thank Prescott for talking me into it."

He hugged her, sat down, and opened his presents from Santa. When Annie stood to gather the paper scattered across the floor, Rafe jumped up and grabbed her arm.

"Wait. You have to open your present from me."

"Okay." Annie sat back down on the couch and he placed a flat box in her lap he'd obviously wrapped himself. Tons of tape covered both ends with a too-short piece of ribbon curled on top.

He waited at her side while she carefully unwrapped the box and lifted the top. Beneath several layers of crisp white tissue lay a framed photograph of Rafe sitting on his bicycle in front of their house at his last birthday party.

Annie covered her mouth with her hand and tried to hide her quivering lips. "This is so sweet, Rafe. How... ?"

"Prescott's a photographer. I mean, he doesn't do it for money but he said he's always loved taking pictures. Do you like it? Why're you crying, Mom?"

She pulled him in for a hug, loving his little boy scent, something between pink bubble gum and sweet grass. "I'm just happy. It means a lot to me that you took the time to give me a gift that means so much to me, Honey."

He shrugged. "It was Prescott's idea."

She swiped the tears from her cheeks and finished picking up the debris that covered the front room floor. Annie loved her little family and she was so thankful Prescott was becoming a part of it.

Prescott called to ask when he could come over, and Annie invited him to join them for breakfast. She whipped eggs with a bit of cream for an omelet, grated cheese on top, put the blueberry muffins in the oven to warm, and brewed the coffee. When Prescott's truck pulled up in front of the house, she asked Rafe to answer the door.

"Merry Christmas," Prescott shouted when he entered the kitchen. He came up behind her and nuzzled her neck. She turned in his arms and kissed him long and hard. He returned to the front room to look at Rafe's gifts.

When Prescott came back to the kitchen, Annie asked, "Do you think he liked the Guitar Hero?"

"You're being facetious." Their gazes met and his smile disappeared. "I want to be a father again, Annie."

A red hot heat crept up Annie's neck to her face, and she scrambled over to the oven to take out the muffins. After she set them on the table, Prescott pulled her down onto his lap.

"Did you hear what I said?"

"I'm sure you'll have more children, Prescott."

"Maybe you could help me fulfill my dream someday," he said, his voice low and sexy.

"A lot is going on right now, Pres. Holidays, the home interview in January, the possibility of Allessandra having her baby prematurely.”

“It’s all good stuff, Annie. I would just like to fit us in there somewhere.”

Rafe ran into the kitchen with a worried expression on his face.

“Need some help?” Prescott said.

Rafe nodded. “Lots.”

Annie jumped off Prescott’s lap. “Breakfast is almost ready, you two, so hurry up, okay?”

Before they sat down to eat, they successfully got the Guitar Hero hooked up and working. Rafe finished his meal and ran back to the front room to play. Annie excused herself to get Prescott’s gift from under the tree.

He removed the wrapping and pulled out the square velvet jewelry box. His eyebrows drew down in a vee as he carefully opened the lid. “It’s beautiful, Annie,” he whispered, pulling out the gold pocket watch.

“Turn it over.”

He read the words engraved on the back then looked up. “I love you too, Annie.” He reached inside his pocket and placed a small box in front of her.

She unwrapped the slim ivory-colored jewelry case and discovered a delicate gold necklace with a small locket dangling at the bottom.

“It’s the most beautiful gift I’ve ever received,” she whispered, carefully drawing out the chain. She opened the locket. Inside lay a tiny picture of Rafe on one side.

“The other side is where you can put a picture of your new baby,” he said.

Her eyes teared up and they exchanged a deep kiss. “This Christmas has been very special for me and Rafe. I loved celebrating it with you.”

“It means a lot to me that you and Rafe would want me to be here, Annie.”

She grasped his hand. “I’ve spent the last few Christmases more depressed than I’ve ever felt in my life. But this holiday, I’m happy. And it’s all your fault. Because of you I’m not missing Cam. I’ve finally let go of the past.”

He looked down at their clasped hands. "I'm enjoying Christmas for the first time in almost three years. Because of you I'm not sprawled on the couch, wallowing in grief."

She leaned closer and kissed him gently on the lips. Their kiss deepened until she pulled away to catch her breath.

"I love you, Prescott."

"And I love you, Annie."

He cupped her jaw in his hand, brought her face inches from his and encased her lips in a warm, soft kiss. His mustache grazed her top lip and hot sensations zinged through her body. His mouth covered hers in sensuous possession and she nipped at his tongue. His hand massaged her breast, his fingers rolled her nipple and she moaned.

Her hand slid slowly up his leg, and the sound of his throaty groan escaped into their kiss. She needed to know how much he wanted her. She wanted him to know how much she needed him. He felt wide and hard and jutted to the side in his pants. She grasped him firmly and clutched his length tightly in her hand, squeezing and releasing.

His sudden gasp surprised her.

"Oh, God," he whispered, leaning his head back. "I didn't mean for that to happen." A guilty expression covered his face and he cupped her chin with his hand.

She pressed her index finger over his lips. "Shhh." She gave him a knowing smile. "Merry Christmas."

He pulled her finger away from his mouth. "Sex isn't a one-way street, Annie."

She shrugged her shoulders. "There are many more hours left in the day."

It was going to be a long Christmas day for her, waiting her turn.

* * * *

They spent a mellow day together and watched Rafe play with his toys. It felt like family. After Annie put Rafe to bed that evening, Prescott pulled her down beside him onto what had become "their" couch.

"I know it's hard to leave Rafe, but the Villa Montalvo has a New Year's Eve dinner with dancing afterward. We could celebrate New Year's Eve together."

Annie took a few moments to think about the logistics of having a night free. "I think I can make it work. Rafe can spend the night at a friend's house or Abby can take care of him for the evening."

"Then we can come back here and sleep in a real bed? Not on the couch," he added with a cute little smirk on his face.

"I think I can arrange that."

CHAPTER TWENTY

Annie made the necessary arrangements for their New Year's Eve date and the next several days flew by. On New Year's Eve day, she treated herself to a manicure, pedicure, and a facial at the local salon in the morning. In the afternoon she searched through her closet and found a dark green, floor-length velvet gown tucked away in the far corner. With tiny white pearls across the bodice, capped sleeves, and a deep vee down the front, it ended just above her naval.

A painful recollection gripped her heart. She'd bought the dress for a party Cam and she were to attend right before he died. She never had a chance to wear it and smiled sadly at the memory. She slipped the dress over her head and slid on the matching heels. Perfect.

The doorbell chimed promptly at seven o'clock. Annie took a deep breath and opened it. Prescott wore a black suit with a white shirt and red tie.

His eyes wide, he blew out a low whistle. "You're gorgeous, Annie."

"Thank you. And you're very handsome, Mr. Beemiller."

He pulled out the gold pocket watch she'd given him, glanced down at it. "It's seven o'clock, and we're all alone for the evening."

She laughed, grabbed her purse, and locked the front door. Prescott laid his hand over hers and escorted her to the Mercedes. When they arrived at the restaurant, valets parked cars in every spot available and inside, almost every table was taken.

The maître d' escorted them to their seats and Prescott placed his hand over hers, interlacing their fingers. "I don't want to say anything to ruin this night for us."

She gave his hand a squeeze and furrowed her brows. "What do you mean? I don't think you could say anything that would ruin our New Year's Eve together."

"Annie, I've never met anyone like you."

"Thank you. But you look so serious. What's this all about?"

"Well, both of us have baggage from the past, but what couples don't, right? I want to move ahead but that's hard to do, given that I'm still married. But it's going on three years and Patti and Dylan are still missing."

"Your attorney and the private investigator are working on the information you need to submit to the judge, right?"

"Yes. And so far the P.I. hasn't stumbled on any clues as to where Patti and Dylan might be. Actually much of what he's doing is repeating what the FBI and police have already done, just covering a wider area.

"But, Annie, my point is, we both still carry around other people in our hearts. And we probably will forever. But that doesn't mean we can't carve out a new life for ourselves."

Annie nodded. "I've done my share of grieving, Prescott. And I can see how, in your case, not knowing is probably more difficult to deal with."

He frowned. "I want to move ahead. I can't grieve forever and there hasn't been one single, solitary clue to give me any hope to hang onto either. It's as if they both disappeared into thin air."

"I'm so sorry, Pres. Yours is one of the saddest situations a person could be in."

"I want us to be a couple."

She sat back in her chair and smiled. "Do you see me going out with anyone else?"

"That's not what I'm implying. I want to know…"

"You want to know if you're the one for me?"

He grinned sheepishly and glanced up at the ceiling. "You're embarrassing me. It sounds so corny when you say it like that. I just want to know if you see our relationship as more than just dating and having some fun in bed."

"I don't sleep with just anyone, Prescott. There hasn't been anyone since Cam." She hesitated. "Could we just let it be for now? I've got so much on my plate with the impending adoption."

"I understand."

"And I have no intention of going out with anyone else."

He grinned. "Neither do I."

They brought dinner to the table, and they lingered over coffee and dessert afterward. The band began to play a slow song, and they stood up to dance. They glided across the floor, Prescott's hands gently caressing her bare back.

At twelve o'clock, he lifted Annie's chin and placed a tender kiss on her lips. "Happy New Year, Annie."

"Happy New Year, Prescott."

They hummed the tune to Auld Lang Syne and as the crowd began to thin out, he stopped. "Would you like to go home now?"

"The rest of the night is ours."

"No distractions, no alarm clock. Just you and me, Annie."

They drove home in silence. Annie was sure they both anxiously anticipated the upcoming evening together. When he closed the front door, he pulled her in for a long, languorous kiss, grasped her under her thighs and lifted her into his arms.

He walked slowly up the stairs to her bedroom where he laid her gently on the bed as if she was a porcelain doll. She leaned back against the pillows and he slid her dress down her hips and let it slide off the bed to the floor.

"With the moon outside the window, you're glowing," he whispered.

In a slow striptease, he removed his clothes and knelt on the bed next to her. Annie grasped him solidly in her hands and caressed him. He dripped kisses along her face and neck, suckled her nipples. Her breathing changed to gasps. She was on the edge.

He pulled her on top of him and she kissed her way down his chest to the deep vee of hair leading below his waist. He moaned as she moved a few inches lower. He cried out her name.

Prescott grabbed her gently under the arms and laid her on top of the pillows. While his lips and tongue caressed her stomach, down to that sweet place of entry, she moaned, reached for the drawer and pulled out a condom. She grasped his shoulders, pulled him back up toward her then opened the packet. After sliding it on, he covered her body with his, gently guiding himself inside.

They rocked together, murmuring soft "I love you's" until Annie reached her peak. Prescott whispered her name again at his final thrust. They lay exhausted in each other's arms and drifted off to sleep.

In the morning, it felt strange to find him sleeping with his head on the pillow next to hers. But Annie was happy and sated. Most importantly, she didn't feel alone.

CHAPTER TWENTY-ONE

The next two months flew by. The county completed their evaluation of her and Rafe and their home. All the background checks were done, and they'd been approved. Prescott completed the nursery and built a fence that enclosed the backyard. All they had to do was wait.

On March third, Annie got a call from Barb from her cell phone. Barb's voice waned in and out, and Annie surmised she was on Route A33 because reception in the hills was spotty at best.

"Barb, I can't hear you."

Barb's voice suddenly got louder, "Allessandra's in a lot of pain. I'm taking her to Sea Cliff Memorial."

Annie gasped, and then covered her mouth with her hand. The day she'd been waiting for had finally arrived. "Is there anything I can do?" She raised her voice to compensate for the static.

"Could you call her doctor, alert him that we're on the way to the hospital?"

"Yes, right away. Tell Allessandra we love her. I'll be there soon."

Annie's hands shook while she made a quick call to the doctor before she pressed in Abby's phone number. Abby agreed to pick up Rafe from school. Annie jumped in the car and left a message for Prescott on his cell phone. Route A33 was nearly deserted. She arrived sooner than expected and walked in just in time to see the nurse wheeling Allessandra down the hall.

Annie ran alongside the wheelchair, and took hold of Allessandra's hand. Allessandra grimaced, the muscles in her face scrunched together in a knot.

"You're going to be fine, Honey." Annie moved the sweat-soaked hair from her forehead with her fingers. "I'll be waiting right here."

Allessandra tried her best to smile, but didn't quite pull it off.

"Thanks for coming, Annie." She inhaled deeply through her nose. "Guess the baby won't be born on St. Patrick's Day, huh?"

Tears crept their way toward Annie's eyelids. "Once they give you the epidural, you won't feel a thing." She kissed Allessandra on the cheek. "See you later."

The nurse wheeled her through the big double doors at the end of the hall.

Allessandra wanted Stacey with her in the Birthing Room so Barb and Annie sat in the waiting room together. The television, tuned to a daytime show based on lie detector tests to determine "who's the baby's daddy", blared in the corner. Close to noon, Prescott rushed in, sat down and pulled Annie in for a hug.

"Thanks for coming." Annie wrapped her arms around him, her face embedded in his warm neck. "I'm not sure when they'll start the epidural. We could be waiting awhile."

His breathing slowed. "I got here as soon as I could." He nodded to Barb. "I knew you'd be nervous. I'm nervous, for God's sake. This whole hospital thing makes me antsy."

Annie loved the fact he didn't hide his feelings. She turned toward Barb. "Would you like to go to the cafeteria? We can eat through our anxiety."

Barb politely declined the offer and Prescott and Annie took the elevator to the cafeteria located on the top floor. They sat holding hands and sipped Cokes, nibbling Cheese Nips, Annie's personal comfort food. Prescott talked about his job in Carpinteria, and Annie shared what she'd accomplished in the baby's room.

After they returned to the waiting room, no more than an hour passed before the doctor ambled down the hallway toward their small group. They stood.

"Allessandra just gave birth to a seven-pound one-ounce baby boy. He came out screaming at the top of his very well-developed lungs."

Annie closed her eyes and smiled. She heard Barb's sigh of relief. Annie was so happy—for her, for Rafe, for everyone who'd experience this new little guy who just entered the world. Annie swayed and Prescott wrapped his arm around her waist.

"Hey, you all right?"

She opened her eyes and whispered, "I'm okay, just grateful. When can we see Allessandra, doctor?"

"She's resting comfortably in the Postpartum Room. She's a little emotional right now. The baby's been taken to the Newborn Nursery." He smiled. "You're welcome to see him if you'd like. Just go to the main desk there." He gestured down the hallway. "The nurses are aware that you're the adoptive parent." He turned and jogged away.

They walked to the nursery. Annie didn't know what she was expecting, but when the nurse pointed to the Dawson baby in the clear plastic bassinet, Annie burst into tears.

The baby was beautiful, with lots of black hair inherited from his father, she assumed, and he quietly sucked on one of his fingers. Allessandra decided she wasn't going to nurse. The bonding would be too overpowering and ill-advised for a woman who wasn't keeping her child. Annie experienced first-hand what it felt like to breast feed, and Annie and Allessandra had discussed it. Although Annie didn't try to influence Allessandra's decision, she'd opted against it.

"He's... perfect," Annie whispered and shook her head. "I can't believe it."

She turned to look at Prescott through the glass partition. Prescott smiled and Annie walked out into the hallway.

Prescott met her at the doorway, put his arm around her shoulders and gave her a tight squeeze. "He's got a lot of hair, huh?"

Annie smiled at Prescott. "And he's going to be ours. I'm so excited."

Barb patted Annie on the back. "You'll have to tell Rafe he has a baby brother."

"He'll be so happy. He told me the other day, he'll be the man of the house now."

They all shared a laugh. Prescott leaned down and kissed the top of her head. "You'll have to tell him he's got to help you out with this little guy in order to earn that title."

"Oh, I think he's looking forward to it, but he hasn't a clue what he's volunteered for. His enthusiasm will probably wear off soon enough."

Prescott glanced at his watch. "It's getting late. Since Allessandra's still with Stacey in the Postpartum Room, maybe we should come back tomorrow to visit her."

Barb decided to wait for Stacey, and Prescott and Annie agreed to head back to Brandiss. They walked through the parking lot to their cars and Prescott pulled Annie in for a hug. "Want to meet back at your place?"

Annie looked up at him, tears imminent. "I'd like that."

They got into their cars and headed home. Annie picked up Rafe at Abby's place and Prescott pulled his truck in the driveway behind her.

When Prescott came around to the passenger side of the car, Rafe jumped out and they high-fived each other.

"Let's have a celebration dinner," Prescott said.

Rafe smiled. "Cool. Whose birthday is it?"

Prescott's eyes widened.

Annie smiled. "Don't worry. I was just about to tell him."

"Tell me what?" Rafe said, looking from his mom to Prescott and back.

"Allessandra had her baby a few hours ago."

"Was it a boy?" Rafe's eyebrows shot up, his eyes wide.

Prescott smiled and Annie rolled her eyes. "Yes, it's a boy, Rafe," she said.

Rafe raised his hand to give Prescott another high-five and Annie laughed and shook her head. "Come inside and I'll fix dinner."

After they ate, they watched *Artificial Intelligence*. Annie let Rafe stay up a little later than usual then tucked him in bed and started down the stairs.

Prescott met her half way. His arms surrounded her waist, pulled her toward him and engaged her mouth in a sensuous kiss.

"You were quiet tonight," he whispered.

"I'm afraid."

"Afraid of what exactly?"

She dropped her gaze, and he pushed her head up with his finger.

"That she'll change her mind," she mumbled.

"You're thinking too much, Annie. You need to get your mind off this."

He turned her around, gently pushed her back up the stairs and guided her toward the bedroom. She walked through the doorway and he closed it gently behind him.

Within moments she'd completely lost herself in his embrace and kisses. His sexual prowess ignited her like no other man she'd been with and she travelled out of today, totally forgetting about tomorrow.

CHAPTER TWENTY-TWO

The next day, Prescott and Annie met at the hospital at noon. They greeted each other in the lobby and took the elevator to the third floor.

When they entered Allessandra's room, she was crying quietly on Stacey's shoulder. Stacey rubbed her back and murmured words Annie couldn't distinguish. She was in the middle of saying, "I feel so bad about…" when they both looked up as Annie and Prescott entered the room.

"Is anything wrong, or is it just post-partum blues?" Annie asked, feeling as if she'd interrupted something secret between the two girls.

Allessandra wiped the tears away with her fingers. "Yeah. Post-partum whatever."

"When are they going to release you and the baby?"

Allessandra forced a half-smile. "I'm eating and drinking, and Jack's had two bottles already so I think we'll be released tomorrow morning."

The conversation screeched to a halt. Annie stared with her mouth open, jaw hanging down, eyes wide. What was going on? A hot blush traveled up her neck to her face.

She'd given the baby a name?

Annie tried to find her calm voice and ended up half-whispering, "You said you weren't going to name the baby. You and I discussed this, remember? You said it was my choice. That's what we agreed on."

Annie glanced at Prescott. He, too, had a stunned expression on his face.

"I know that, Annie," Allessandra said with more than a little irritation in her voice. "But when I saw him in the nursery this morning... I don't know. The least I can do is give him a name. And it's my dad's name. Doesn't change anything."

Maybe Annie was making more out of this than necessary so she tamped down her anger before answering. "Okay. I like the name Jack. I could get used to it." She paused to reel in her emotions. "About tomorrow. I'm supposed to call Mr. Mayer. He'll meet us here before they release you. You and I can sign the necessary papers. Is that still okay?" For several reasons, Annie wasn't exactly sure what Allessandra's answer would be.

"Yeah, yeah. We'll do the deal then go our separate ways."

Allessandra was being rather flippant about such an important issue, but maybe it was a form of self-preservation to shield herself from feeling she was abandoning her child.

"I'll call you after I've spoken with him to tell you when he'll be here," Annie said.

Prescott and Annie said goodbye and walked to their cars without saying a word. When they reached the Mercedes, he put his hands on her shoulders and turned her toward him. "Don't make a big deal out of this. It's all new for her. She doesn't know how to act."

Annie shook her head and stared at the ground.

Prescott lifted her chin with his finger. "She hasn't changed her mind. Not if she's agreeing to meet with the attorney tomorrow morning. Who's to say what either of us would do in her place."

"I hope you're right. This is exactly why I'm so afraid. She's only seventeen and changing her mind wouldn't be a surprise. It was such a surprise when she called the baby Jack. She completely blindsided me."

He frowned.

"Maybe she thinks it's the least she could do for the baby before she gives him to me."

"That's my girl." He smiled. "It's a hard thing she's doing, Annie. Don't expect her to go through it with a smile on her face, or to act like a grown-up because she's not one."

They kissed goodbye and he headed to work. Annie drove home, thinking too much, mulling over every nuance of Allessandra's behavior, worrying herself sick with what-if's.

Luckily, Prescott made use of his free time on the two previous weekends to complete the work on the nursery.

But the next morning a gray cloud still hung over Annie's head. By giving the baby a name, Allessandra had tainted Annie's excitement. She tried her best to downplay the episode, but it invaded her every thought. But she did her best not to let it get her down.

Prescott headed to work and Annie drove to the hospital to meet Mr. Mayer at ten a.m. Allessandra, dressed and ready to go, didn't say much when Mr. Mayer arrived with the documents for them to sign. The nurses asked Annie to meet them in another wing of the hospital when they finished the paperwork so Jack and Annie could get ready to leave.

Tears coursed down Allessandra's cheeks and her hand shook as she held the pen above the legal papers.

"I'll stand outside and give you some privacy," Mr. Mayer said.

Annie nodded and sat in the chair next to Allessandra.

"Are you having second thoughts?" Annie asked.

Allessandra's lips quivered. "I didn't think it would be this hard."

Annie put her arm around Allessandra's shoulders. "I know I've said it before, but this is an extraordinary thing you're doing and one of the most unselfish acts I think any woman can do. Rafe and I are so thankful you've chosen us to be Jack's new family and we'll give him all the love he will ever want."

Allessandra met Annie's gaze, unwavering, her eyes wide and glassy.

"And this is an open adoption, Allessandra. That means you and Rafe and I agree that you'll be part of Jack's life, if you want to be, as much as you want to be. If you just want me to send you pictures of him, I could do that. If you want to come to his birthday parties or visit whenever you want, that's fine, too.

"This doesn't have to be the end of your relationship with any of us. But again, that's up to you. And whatever amount of contact you decide on, that's okay with us."

Allessandra stared down at the paper and flipped to the last page, the pen inches above the signature line. She placed the tip of the pen on the black line and scribbled her name, stood, pushed back the chair and ran out of the room.

Annie signed the documents and handed them to Mr. Mayer on her way out then walked to the other wing of the hospital. Her car was ready with the car seat and diaper bag. The nurses gave her a few bottles of baby formula to take with her until she got settled at home. She was anxious to see Rafe when he arrived home from school and Prescott was coming over later that evening.

Annie was so excited, she couldn't stop talking to the baby on the ride back to Brandiss. But she just couldn't shake the funny feeling about Allessandra naming the baby. And, though she understood her hesitation about signing the papers, it all added to her anxiety about the adoption.

However, now that she'd have two children, she certainly wouldn't have spare time to worry about her state of mind. She had to face the fact there was nothing she could do about it and move forward.

Rafe came home soon after Annie put Jack down for a nap. Rafe ran into the house, eager to see his baby brother. They tip-toed into the nursery where Jack lay on his stomach, making little sucking noises with his tiny red lips.

Rafe stood next to the crib, smiling. "I've never been this close to a baby before."

Annie's heart felt so full it was about to burst. She had the most wonderful son. And now another. "You can hold him as soon as he wakes up."

Rafe shook his head, not taking his eyes off Jack. "Nah. Remember what I told you? About what my friends said about baby barf? That's totally gross."

Annie laughed under her breath and tried not to make too much noise. "You could read books to him. He'll learn to love the sound of your voice and begin to recognize you."

Rafe stared at the baby, as though mesmerized. "What're we gonna name him?"

Annie expected this and had already prepared what she was going to say. "I wanted to talk to you about that, Rafe." He glanced away from the crib, eyebrows knit together. "You know Allessandra's father and mother were killed in a plane accident. She wanted to name the baby Jack in memory of her dad. Would that be all right with you?"

He shrugged. "She told me how her mom and dad died. That's messed up."

Annie took hold of Rafe's hand and they tiptoed out of the nursery. Rafe never ceased to impress her with his agreeable nature and since Cam's death, he'd matured beyond his years. She guessed death could do that to a young boy. And Rafe was so jazzed he wouldn't be the only kid in the house any longer, now elevated to the status of "the older brother."

That evening, Prescott dropped by. As the two of them stood over the crib watching the baby sleep, he pulled her in for a hug and whispered, "These are the times I remember with Dylan. I only had nine months with him. I never got to see him walk, never heard him say his first word. No first birthday party. It's never stopped being a nightmare."

She kissed the underside of his chin, worked her way up to his lips. "Jack's in our lives now, Pres. He'll never take the place of Dylan, but you can share him with us. I want him to be part of your life as well."

"I know that, and I don't mean to be a downer. It's just me venting, I guess. Sorry."

She gave him a little shake. "Don't ever apologize for your feelings about Dylan. I want you to share your thoughts with me. No secrets between us. Promise?"

"Promise."

They quietly stepped out of the bedroom and said goodnight. It had been a very long day. Annie was emotionally exhausted, and tonight would be a long one, feeding the baby every few hours.

As the weeks flew by, Jack got fatter and happier. Annie enjoyed her time alone with him and Jack learned to smile at her and recognized who she was. He knew Rafe as well because he often read books to Jack while showing him the pictures.

Prescott finished painting the outside of the house and was remodeling the ancient two-car garage. He took time out to visit the baby every day. Annie often found him in the nursery holding Jack or leaning over the crib as he shook a rattle or showed him a new toy he purchased.

April's weather turned mild and pleasant. Annie sat on the porch swing and was reading a book when the mail lady waved to her as she approached their mailbox under the pergola.

Annie ran down the stairs, grabbed the bundle, and looked

through the mail when she came upon a legal-sized envelope from Mr. Mayer. She slipped her finger under the flap and opened it. It was his letterhead, but it wasn't a bill. It was titled "Revocation of Consent for Adoption."

Her knees gave out beneath her and she dropped down onto the swing seat. She read and re-read the letter.

Allessandra had changed her mind.

Allessandra had decided on a six-month period in which to make her final decision and she could revoke her previous agreement during that time. Annie hadn't heard from her since she'd given birth but that didn't surprise Annie. She figured Allessandra was busy planning her trip with Stacey after graduation and getting on with her life.

Annie burst into tears. Her heart felt as though it was being ripped out of her chest. Her head throbbed. Waves of nausea washed over her. She ran inside, grabbed the phone and pressed the numbers for Mr. Mayer's office and was immediately put through.

"You received my letter, Mrs. Davidson," he said in a monotone.

"I had absolutely no idea Allessandra was having any doubts concerning the adoption. Isn't there anything I can do?"

"By California law, she has the right to change her mind with regard to your adopting her child any time during the six-month period following the child's birth. Young girls have a change of heart after giving birth. The baby becomes real to them and they can't go through with it."

Annie kept shaking her head. This was not happening. "How will she take care of him if she's working and going to school?" She was crying so hard she could hardly get the words out and gasped for breath between sentences. "What am I supposed to do now?"

"When I met with Allessandra last week she said she's going to take a break from school and acquire her G.E.D. later. She'll continue living with her aunt and cousin, and will work the three to ten p.m. shift at the supermarket. During her working hours, her aunt and cousin will care for the child. She believes she can do this."

It took all her self-control not to throw the phone across the room. "What happens next?" she said, her throat clogged with tears.

"On Monday, May fifth, you'll have to bring Jack to my office. Allessandra will pick him up here. You don't have to be here when she arrives. You could leave him in my care for the fifteen minutes between your appointments."

"What time should I be at your office?"

"Is one o'clock convenient for you?"

Annie closed her eyes and tried her best to answer his question without choking on the words. "I'll be there."

May fifth. Cinco de Mayo. Her birthday.

Happy Birthday to me.

CHAPTER TWENTY-THREE

She needed to talk to Prescott. If he wasn't working at her house, he'd be out talking to potential clients, or in the store purchasing materials. Either way, it wasn't Annie's style to interrupt his work day. But she desperately needed to hear his voice.

He answered immediately, and she could do nothing but cry. She tried to form coherent words, but they refused to come out. She didn't know where to start.

"Annie, is that you?" he asked in a loud voice, but Annie could barely hear him over the hum of his truck's diesel engine.

"I got a letter from Mr. Mayer. Oh God, Prescott. She changed her mind."

"Wait. Who changed their mind? Annie, what are you talking about?"

"Allessandra changed her mind about my adopting Jack. I have to bring him back to Mr. Mayer's office. On May fifth. On my birthday. Prescott, I'm dying inside."

"Shit. I'll be there in five minutes."

It seemed only seconds passed before his truck pulled up in front of the house. Heavy footsteps resounded on the front porch before he yanked the front door open.

He sat next to Annie and pulled her into his arms. "When did this happen?"

"I got a letter from Mr. Mayer today."

"Did you talk to him?"

She nodded. "To... set up... the appointment," she said between sobs, "for returning Jack... to Allessandra."

"I had no idea, Annie."

She pulled away. "She hasn't spoken with you about anything?"

He shook his head. "Of course not. I would have told you. I

haven't seen her since that day in the hospital after she had the baby. I don't understand what's going on with her any more than you do."

His eyes appeared as misty as hers. "She's taking my baby away from me. I don't know what I'm going to do without him."

He wrapped his arms around her and held her close. "Believe me, I know what it's like for someone to yank your child away from you."

Annie closed her eyes and cried while Prescott rocked her in his arms, her body so weak, she didn't know if she could stand. But she had to pick up Rafe from school. And she had to tell Rafe his baby brother was leaving forever.

Cameron died two years ago. And now this? Life was unfair sometimes. But Annie was glad she had Prescott to lean on. She was grateful for his support. He stayed with Jack while she drove to Rafe's school.

After Rafe shut the car door, he frowned. "What's the matter, Mom? Your face looks funny. Did you get my progress report in the mail? Did I get a bad grade?"

Annie shook her head. "It's not that, Rafe." She took a deep breath. "Remember when we talked about the adoption process and I told you Allessandra has six months to change her mind about us adopting Jack?" He nodded. "She decided she wants to keep Jack after all. And you and I have to honor her decision. It's the law. We have to give Jack back to her."

His lower lip trembled, and tears dripped down his cheeks. Annie draped her arm over his shoulders and hugged him close. His body shook with sobs.

She drove the few blocks home in silence, clutching him around the shoulders with one arm. They arrived home and after she opened the front door, he ran past her, up the stairs, and slammed the door to his room.

Prescott joined her in the foyer. "Should we talk to him?" he asked, his voice filled with distress.

"He'll be asleep in a few minutes."

He lifted his eyebrows.

"That's what he does."

"You mean when he's upset?"

She nodded. "I've got to sit down." Annie motioned towards the front room. "We'll talk in there."

They sat on the couch, and she leaned her head back and stared at the ceiling. "Rafe had a friend in Sausalito who got a puppy. A chocolate lab named Mocha. Rafe loved that dog. He helped feed her, took her for a walk every day with his pal. He'd take care of Mocha any time the family went on vacation. He felt he was part owner of the dog."

Annie turned her head to face him. "One day Mocha was hit by a car and Rafe was devastated. He slept for hours. When Cam died, he did the same thing. I imagine it's the way his mind reacts to emotional stress."

He reached for her hand. "How do you deal with emotional stress?"

She shut her eyes and wished this were a nightmare. Perhaps she'd wake up later and this would all have been a dream. "I'm just the opposite. I don't sleep. I can't eat. Right now I feel physically ill." Tears seeped from under her closed eyelids. "I can't believe this is happening."

He pulled her closer to his side and Annie laid her head on his chest, dampening his shirt with her tears.

"I want to help you get through this, Annie. I won't leave you."

"I've lost control of my life, Pres. Jack will be wrested away from us forever, and I can't do a damn thing to stop it." She fisted her hands in her lap. "My son's heart is being torn apart, and I can't fix it."

Prescott pulled her back into his firm embrace and rubbed her back as her body shook with silent sobs. "Make the most of the few days you have left with Jack," he whispered. "Rafe could take some time off from school. You can go for walks, maybe a long drive, spend quality time with the baby before he has to leave."

"You'll come with us?"

He kissed the top of her head. "I'll be right by your side, for as long as you need me."

Those last days with Jack were bittersweet. They managed to laugh a little. And cry a lot. They took him for long walks in his stroller, went for drives through the hills, and Rafe pointed out the cows on the hillsides.

Prescott and Annie agreed Rafe shouldn't accompany them to Mr. Mayer's office. It would be devastating for Annie, and Rafe was only eleven years old. It would be too traumatic for him.

On May fourth, Prescott and Annie sat at the kitchen table. She was counting down the hours until the following day, dreading every second of time's passing.

"Are you going to talk with Allessandra at the attorney's office?" Prescott asked.

Annie shrugged. "It wouldn't do any good. I can't change her mind. She was the one who was desperate for me to adopt Jack. She did her best to convince me it was the best thing for her and the baby. So if she wants him back, she must be damn serious."

"You're probably right."

"She and I spent hours discussing what we wanted for the baby's future. She wanted to travel, meet her dream man, have kids when she was older. She and I were close, really close. I'm so hurt she couldn't talk to me about any doubts she was having. She and I had a special bond."

He reached over and took hold of both her hands. "She's eighteen years old, Annie. Do you remember what it was like to be that age? One day I was sure about something and the next day, I'd change my mind. And I thought I was being totally normal."

Annie recalled her high school years, which put a small smile on her face. "I guess that rules out her having developed a case of amnesia and forgetting everything she told me over the last several months, huh?"

He leaned in and kissed her forehead. "You'll get past this, Annie. We'll get past this. Together."

Annie nodded. With her whole heart, she hoped he was right.

CHAPTER TWENTY-FOUR

May fifth dawned bright and beautiful. Instead of waking his mother with shouts of "Happy Birthday" as in the past, Rafe didn't come into her bedroom, had no creative gift he'd made in class, no morning kiss. She wanted to crawl under the covers and never come out. It was seven in the morning, and Annie was already dreading the day.

She explained to Rafe that children weren't allowed at this legal proceeding, and he believed her. When it came time for him to say goodbye to Jack, she couldn't watch. Moments later he ran out of the nursery, tears streaming down his cheeks. Annie took Jack out of his crib, held him in her arms and walked down the stairs with him for the last time.

Prescott waited in his truck. Annie grabbed her purse and dragged her body outside. After she dropped Rafe at Abby's inn, where she'd arranged for him to spend quiet time with Abby for the day, Annie and Prescott drove to Sea Cliff. Jack lay in his car seat, clothes and bottles and formula in the diaper bag, the three of them heading off under the shining sun for their final moments together.

Once they arrived at Mr. Mayer's office, there were no papers to sign. Annie just had to leave Jack and walk out the door. Mr. Mayer made it as simple as possible. He didn't ask how they were doing. *Oh, great, thank you for asking.* He showed them into his office, left them alone and allowed them the opportunity to say goodbye.

It took every last bit of Annie's strength to kiss Jack for the last time. She whispered, "I'll love you forever," and it felt as if she was saying her last words to a dying person. But the only person dying right now was Annie. She hoped Jack would adjust to living with Allessandra, but that was out of her hands now and out of her control. She had to let it go. She had to let him go.

Prescott and Annie walked slowly back to the truck. Prescott hugged her close to his side as she cried, leaning against him for support as they made their way through the parking lot. As they came up to the passenger side of the truck, a car door opened next to them. There stood Allessandra.

"Oh... Annie, hi," she said, obviously surprised.

She didn't have the decency to confront Annie about changing her mind and now she was talking to her?

Annie opened the door of the truck and climbed in without saying a word.

Prescott must not have felt the same way about getting out of there so quickly because his voice rang out, loud and clear.

"Why didn't you tell Annie you changed your mind?" He sounded as bitter as Annie felt.

"I thought a lot about it, Pres, and I just can't do it. I can't give up my kid. I missed him so badly. My mom and dad are both dead. Jack's the only family I've got. I can have what Annie has with Rafe. Barb and Stacey will help me out with babysitting when I'm at work."

Prescott's voice rose higher than before. "I get it. But you could have at least told her to her face. It was like getting a Dear John letter."

Annie never heard him so upset.

"Not after everything I'd said about wanting her to adopt Jack," she cried. "She would think I'd been lying to her all along. And I wasn't."

Through the open window of the truck Annie heard Allessandra crying. Annie understood what Allessandra meant about having family and she couldn't fault her rationale. However, the way she'd gone about it had hurt Annie so much.

Prescott jumped in the truck, turned the key in the ignition, and skidded out of the parking lot. Annie was bone-weary and sick to her stomach. She just wanted to get home.

They drove to Brandiss without a word between them. It was over. Discussing it wasn't going to change a thing.

They arrived back at the house around lunch time, but Annie couldn't eat. The piece of toast she forced down at breakfast felt as if it was still stuck in her throat.

She had to be strong for Rafe, stay focused on something besides

Jack's absence. She was determined to make it through this horrific episode to the other side, just as she had after Cam's death. And she needed to be there for her son. Now more than ever. He had just recovered from his father's death and now this.

They just walked in the door when Annie turned to Prescott. "Will you help me get the things out of the nursery?"

His hands grasped her arms and pulled her in toward him. "You don't have to do this now."

"Yes, I do. And I'm going to do it right now, with or without your help." Annie wrenched out of his arms and rushed up the stairs. She could hear his footsteps behind her.

"Annie! Stop!"

She stood at the nursery, her head resting against the door, trying not to cry. She couldn't believe she had any tears left.

"It's okay," he whispered and surrounded her in his embrace. "I'll help you through this. I promise."

She turned around and clutched him in her arms. "It'll be easier for us to deal with losing Jack without having all of his things around to remind us."

"We'll put them in the attic."

A tear escaped down her cheek. "I couldn't give all of his favorite toys to Allessandra. And I refuse to pretend he was never a part of our lives. That would be wrong. I want to remember him." Her voice caught in her throat. More tears streaked down her cheeks.

"I know. I still have some of Dylan's toys on top of my dresser at the house. I don't ever want to forget him, either."

They put the few remaining toys in a cardboard box, took apart the crib, added a couple of tiny outfits and baby blankets, various knickknacks, and brought everything to the attic.

After that, they drove to the Inn to pick up Rafe, and the moment he got in the truck, Annie could tell he wasn't doing well. She turned around and pasted a smile on her face. "Would you like to go for pizza? It's my birthday, you know."

No reaction. He stared out the side window. Several seconds passed before he mumbled, "I don't care."

To be honest, Annie didn't care either.

Prescott twisted around in his seat. "Maybe we could wait until this weekend to go out."

Rafe shrugged. "Doesn't matter."

His short, half-audible answers, reminiscent of the months after Cam died, frightened Annie to the core. If she couldn't get him to talk about anything, she couldn't help him recover. But she'd be there for him whenever he felt like opening up.

When Prescott pulled up in front of the house, she suddenly felt exhausted. "I'm going to take a nap. Could you just drop us off?"

"I'll call you later." He leaned over and kissed her goodbye.

When Annie suggested they watch television and eat dinner, Rafe didn't answer. So she turned on the TV, selected the Nickelodeon channel, and sat next to him on the couch, her arm around his small shoulders. They both fell asleep.

Annie woke up first, nauseous and lethargic. She hadn't eaten much all day, and her stomach churned. She tip-toed into the kitchen to fix dinner. Rafe needed to eat and she should eat as well. Either way, she couldn't feel any worse than she did now.

Annie fixed tomato soup with grilled cheese sandwiches, one of Rafe's favorite meals. She usually enjoyed them also, but could hardly keep it down. After she put the dishes in the dishwasher, she sat with him to watch a Disney show, feeling more weary than she could ever remember, the emotional drain immeasurable.

When the program ended, she walked him upstairs to his bedroom, happy to see the nursery door shut. She climbed into bed and fell asleep, the only way she could stop thinking about how much she missed Jack. He'd changed their family life in such a short time. And now he was gone.

CHAPTER TWENTY-FIVE

June meant summer was on the horizon, marking Annie's favorite time of year. Flowers bloomed, and it was the season to plant vegetables. This time, however, she'd be doing the job solo, without Allessandra's help.

Most of the time she felt in a daze, going about her daily activities like a robot. It all felt so unreal. Every day she walked around in a fog.

While sitting at the dinner table one evening with Rafe, she asked, "School okay?"

He pushed his plate aside and leaned his elbows on the table. "I miss him. Kinda like how I miss Dad. Like Jack died, too."

Annie pursed her lips and tried her best not to burst into tears. She was so, so tired of crying. "It feels that way to me, too, Honey. Even though Jack lives just a few blocks from us, we don't get to see him."

"Will I ever see him again?" he said, his brows drawn down into a deep vee.

She rubbed his back with her hand, kissed the side of his soft brown head of hair. "I'm sure we'll see him someday. I just don't think it's a good idea to do that right now."

He covered his face with both hands and cried, big gulping sobs that tore at her heart. All she could do was hold him, murmuring everything would be okay and they'd get past this.

As the days rolled by, an occasional smile appeared on his face, he told Annie stories about his teachers and friends again, rode his bike around more often, laughed.

Prescott continued working on the house. He was almost finished with the renovation. Prescott and Rafe both seemed to weather the aftermath of Jack's departure better than Annie.

She still felt lethargic and weak, had no appetite, barely managed to finish meals. And her conversations with Prescott had been reduced to small talk.

When she walked past him on her way up the front stairs one day, he reached out for her arm. "Annie, stop." He gently guided her to the bottom of the stairs and put his arms around her. She rested her head on the soft flannel of his shirt. "You're avoiding me. We haven't said more than a few words to each other since Jack left."

She closed her eyes and wished to God they weren't having this conversation. She didn't want to deal with the sadness. She was mentally wiped out. "There's nothing to say. Rafe and I talked about it and he's doing pretty well."

He pulled back to look her square in the face. "What about you, Annie? How are you doing?"

She turned away. She didn't want him to see her expression, devastation written all over her face. She was living on the edge.

He lifted her chin with his fingers and stared into her eyes.

"I can't stop thinking about him," she cried. "He's just around the corner. I want to hold him again, feel his chubby fingers grasp my thumb. I can't eat. I can't sleep." She was so damn frustrated with her life, she wanted to scream at the top of her lungs at the world.

He pulled her down to sit on the bottom step and put his arm around her shoulders. "You should see a doctor. Maybe they'll give you an antidepressant or an appetite stimulant or something to help you sleep. I don't know. When was the last time you had a physical?"

She shrugged. "Right after Cam died."

"I'm not a doctor, but a lot of your symptoms are signs of depression, Annie." He gave her shoulders a squeeze. "Or maybe you're anemic. You said you aren't eating much. You might be deficient. It couldn't hurt to make an appointment."

She nodded. "You're right." She gave him a small smile, and he kissed her on the forehead before letting her up.

Abby gave her the name of her physician in Sea Cliff, and Annie made an appointment for mid-June. That would give her enough time to feel better, and she could cancel it before the day arrived. However, she was getting worse, a steady decline.

When the day arrived, Prescott asked if he could keep her company during the drive to see the doctor, but she wanted to be alone, so she declined his invitation. She had a headache, her stomach was upset, and she felt anxious and nervous. Different day, same symptoms.

The doctor's office was located a block from Sea Cliff Memorial Hospital. After notifying the receptionist of her arrival, Annie filled out the requisite forms, and then went through the motions of looking through a *Health* magazine. A few minutes later, the nurse ushered her into a room where she undressed and waited for the doctor.

Dr. Claire Jackson was about Annie's age, in her early thirties. She greeted Annie with a smile, and took an extensive history of her health and current symptoms. After having Annie's blood drawn, the doctor asked her what was going on in her life and Annie explained about Jack and the adoption.

She commiserated with Annie and placed her hand over Annie's. "Mrs. Davidson, you've been through quite an ordeal, losing a child you were hoping to adopt. I'm not surprised you're physically drained, given the emotional upheaval you've experienced. Combined with the lack of proper diet and little sleep, I would expect you to feel ill. Now, why don't you get dressed and meet me in my office when you're ready."

When Annie finished dressing, the nurse escorted her into Dr. Jackson's office. When the doctor entered the room, she closed the door and took a seat at the desk. The doctor leaned forward and tapped her finger on the buff-colored file. "You're pregnant, Mrs. Davidson."

"Pregnant?" Annie shook her head and tried to absorb this news.

"You're about three months along. Due date around December eighth."

"Can you tell me the date of conception?"

She studied her notes. "My guess would be in early March."

Annie thought back to that month and smiled.

"Does that make sense to you?"

Annie nodded. "Yes, it does. That was the day Jack was born. The baby I was supposed to adopt. That night we didn't use protection."

"Are you happy about this?"

"My first husband and I were trying to have another baby when Rafe was about eight years old but it just wasn't happening. Around the time I was going to make an appointment with a fertility specialist, Cam was killed." She shook her head. "And now? The one time I get carried away and don't use contraception, I get pregnant. So this is certainly a surprise. But a nice one."

Dr. Jackson gave Annie the name of a female gynecologist in the Sea Cliff area, and Annie walked out to her car. Her hands were shaking so hard, she couldn't turn the key in the ignition.

The edges of her lips quirked up in a smile. Pregnant. With Prescott's baby.

She wasn't sure what Prescott's reaction would be since they weren't married. And she had no idea how to approach Rafe with the news, though she was sure he'd be happy to have a baby brother or sister, especially after the adoption debacle.

When Annie arrived home, Prescott was painting the trim on one side of the house. The outside looked like a picture from House Beautiful.

He climbed down from the scaffolding. "What happened at the doctor's?"

"I'll explain it all to you as soon as we get inside. Would you like something to drink?"

"Sure." He followed her into the kitchen and sat at the table.

After placing two steaming mugs of coffee on the table, Annie took a deep breath. "Dr. Jackson gave me a thorough exam, drew some blood. I'm not anemic."

"Well, that's a good thing. Did she say it was depression? Did she prescribe any medication?"

"Well, no," she said and ran her finger around the edge of her mug. "Actually, I have to stay away from any drugs." She looked up at him. "I'm pregnant."

His face went suddenly blank. She was terrified he was going to walk out the door, out of her life, or volunteer to take her to the nearest abortion clinic.

He stood up and turned toward the window. Several seconds passed before he bent down and helped her stand so he could hold her in his arms. He gave her a hug, pulled away... and smiled.

"You've made me the happiest man on the planet," he said. He kissed her and pulled back with a quizzical expression on his face. "You wouldn't joke about something like this, would you?"

Annie drew back as if offended. "No. I mean, yes. Yes, it's true."

He glanced down at the table. "You shouldn't be drinking coffee."

She tilted her head and smiled. "I know that, Prescott. I switched to decaf over a month ago. I read how it can raise your stress level so I went cold turkey. Apparently, stress wasn't the only thing making me feel sick." She slumped into her chair with a sigh. "Are you happy?"

He sat down and grasped her hands. "Do you really have to ask me? When are you due?"

"December eighth."

"Wow. A Christmas baby," he murmured, shaking his head. "God, I love you. All I want to do is make a family with you, Rafe, and our baby."

Annie cocked one eyebrow. "You can't do that, Prescott. You're still married to Patti."

"I spoke with my attorney, Mr. Callahan, and it shouldn't be much longer before he presents his material to the judge."

"And still no clues to their whereabouts?"

"No. But if the judge grants the service of publication, that takes six weeks. After that, hopefully I can proceed with the divorce. And because it's obviously uncontested, it shouldn't take more than a couple of months." He knelt down in front of her, still holding her hands, and gazed into her eyes. "Then will you marry me, Annie Davidson?" He pulled her up and enveloped her in his arms.

Annie ran her finger over his lips and smiled. "Yes, I'll marry you, Prescott Beemiller."

He took her face in his hands and kissed her, leaving her breathless. "Let's live together, Annie. Everyone in town knows about Patti and Dylan anyway, so I don't think there would be any sort of backlash about us living under the same roof."

"Cam and I lived together for a few months before we were married, but we already set the date for our wedding. This is different."

"Oh, man, I'm sorry. We have to think of Rafe. That was selfish of me. What kind of an example would we be giving him?"

"What I think is, the baby needs a full-time father. And you can't be there for the baby or Rafe or me, if we're living apart. If the process for getting your divorce takes longer than you think, of course I could do it alone, but the baby would miss out on having you here, and you'd miss out on all the day-to-day things that happen unexpectedly—first words, first steps."

"I agree with you, but... ."

"You're the first man Rafe's let into his life since Cam died. He loves you, Pres. It's more important to show him by our example what it's like to truly love someone, through the hard times, as well as the good times."

She wrapped her arms around his neck, and stared into his gorgeous hazel eyes. "I think it's the best way to handle this, given the circumstances. Our baby may be born before the judge grants you a divorce."

"Then as soon as my divorce is final, I want to get married. Even if you're due the very next day."

She laid her head on his chest and closed her eyes. "This is all happening so fast."

"When should we tell Rafe about the baby?"

"Not yet. I'll know when it's time. Let's savor this for a little while. Just the two of us."

"You know your son better than I do."

"I'm happy about the baby. Rafe was so disappointed when we had to give Jack back to Allessandra. This will really help him get over losing him."

"He'll never forget Jack and neither will you. But see, Annie, you can be happy again."

She smiled, took his hand, and walked to the bottom of the stairs. "Let's celebrate."

CHAPTER TWENTY-SIX

Summer break began and Rafe was happier than Annie had seen him since Jack's departure. Prescott and Annie agreed to take this opportunity to add to his good mood. Annie fixed a special dinner for the three of them. They sat at the dining room table where she'd placed a big bowl of spaghetti, a plate of garlic bread, and a salad.

She piled Rafe's plate to the brim with spaghetti. "You'd love to have a baby brother or sister, right sweetie?"

His head jerked up and he scowled. "Why? Is there some other girl who wants to give us her baby then change her mind?"

"No, that's not it at all." Annie knelt down next to him. "I'm going to have a baby, Rafe. You're going to have a new brother or sister."

His brow furrowed. "Do you mean it?" She nodded. "Does this mean Pres is gonna be my new dad?"

She nodded at Prescott.

Prescott cleared his throat, leaned forward and folded his hands on the table. "Rafe, I used to be married to a woman named Patti. I had a son, Dylan. He'd be almost four years old by now."

"You had a son?" Rafe asked. "Did he die?"

"No. I mean, I don't know." Prescott took a deep breath.

"You don't know if Dylan died? Did Patti die?" Rafe asked, looking confused.

Prescott raked his hand through his hair, leveled his gaze at Rafe. "I came home one day and they were both gone. They disappeared."

Rafe glanced at Annie then back at Prescott. He frowned. "What happened to them?"

"The police and the FBI don't know. They're still searching, but they've never found either of them."

Rafe set down his fork, his expression pensive. "Do you still miss them?"

Prescott nodded, his eyes glassy. "Every day of my life, Rafe. I want to marry your mom, but the law says I can't do that until I get a divorce. And that's going to take a few more months."

Rafe nodded. "But do you love my Mom more than Patti?"

Prescott's eyes grew wide, and his mouth opened slightly. A few seconds passed before he answered. "I'll always hold a special place in my heart for Patti but after I met your mom, I fell in love." He turned toward Annie. "She's the most beautiful person both inside and out I've ever met." He glanced back at Rafe. "So, to answer your question, I love your Mom more, Rafe." He drew in a ragged breath. "I think Patti and Dylan are probably dead."

Rafe pushed back his chair and walked over to Prescott, wrapped his arms around his neck. "It's kinda like my Dad. I love him and he's dead. But I love you, too."

Tears rolled down Prescott's cheeks. He patted Rafe on the back and pulled away. "I love you too, Rafe. And if I could marry your mom, I would, in a minute. But we have to wait for the divorce to be completed." He paused. "How would you feel if I moved in with you and your mom?"

Rafe smiled and nodded his head with enthusiasm. "Then I wouldn't be the only guy in the house."

"That's true. And when we have a family vote, we can gang up on your mom."

Rafe laughed and sat back down in his chair. "Can I have a piece of garlic bread?"

Annie nodded. "Of course."

"What kind of baby are you having?" Rafe grabbed another piece of bread off the plate.

"What kind of baby?" Annie said, confused.

"You know. Is it a boy or a girl?"

Annie laughed so hard, her cheeks hurt. Prescott chuckled under his breath.

Annie said, "Well, we don't know if the baby's a boy or a girl." She lifted an eyebrow at Prescott.

Prescott shrugged. "I don't want to know until the baby's born. I love surprises. But hey, I'm only the dad."

Rafe glanced from his mom to Prescott and back. "I want it to be a boy."

Prescott shrugged again. "I don't care, as long as the baby's healthy. What about you, Annie? Boy or girl?"

She grinned. "Listen up, you two. One, it'll be a surprise. I love surprises. Two, I'd love the baby to be a boy or a girl. That's all I'm going to say about it."

Rafe and Prescott looked at each other and laughed.

"Now, why don't you two go watch TV, and I'll clean up?" she said.

She didn't have to ask twice.

* * * *

Several weeks later Annie went to the market and Stacey wasn't working in the bakery as usual.

She walked up to the nearest cashier. "Do you know if Stacey's hours have changed?"

The young man shook his head as he continued scanning the customer's items. "She's out of town and won't be back for a while."

"Is she on vacation?"

He shook his head again. "She went with her cousin on a road trip. They're driving across the U.S."

"Did they take Allessandra's baby with them?"

He stopped, turned toward Annie and sighed in irritation. "Look. I don't even know Stacey that well, ma'am. And I don't know if they took a baby with them. Sorry." He returned to helping the customer, showing Annie his back.

"Sorry to have bothered you. Thank you for your help."

She walked to the car and sat staring out the windshield. Allessandra wouldn't bring Jack with her on a cross-country journey, would she? If she wanted to run wild, run free, across the entire continent of the United States, she'd do it without Jack. But would she abandon Jack so soon after getting him back? And what about returning to school?

Between pulling out of the parking lot and turning toward home, Annie decided to visit Barb, to see if Allessandra had taken Jack with her. It had been months since she'd seen him. She'd forgiven

Allessandra for not talking to her before she changed her mind. Though Annie would miss Jack every day for the rest of her life, she was focused on her own pregnancy. She felt ready to see Jack again, without it tearing her apart.

She parked in front of Barb's house, walked up the front steps and rang the doorbell. She could hear music playing softly through the screen door and the sounds of someone talking on the phone. She rang the bell a second time.

Barb rushed around the corner, carrying Jack in her arms, a phone cradled under her chin. She motioned for Annie to come in, and pointed toward the couch. Annie sat down, and Barb placed Jack in her lap, mouthing she'd be off the phone in a second.

This was not what Annie expected. She wasn't prepared to hold Jack on her lap while he stared up at her with those big brown saucer eyes, drooling all over his undershirt, smiling his toothless grin.

Annie still loved him as much as she had the last time she saw him. It was as though she turned back the clock, refreshing every emotion she'd been trying to lay aside. She kissed his chubby cheeks and swiped away the errant tears coursing down her face.

Annie could hear Barb in the back somewhere, her voice raised. "I told you I'd take care of it and I will. I'll call you back tonight and tell you what he says."

Barb returned to the front room, plopped down on the far end of the couch and let out a deep breath. "Good grief."

"I was at the market today and I didn't see Stacey in the bakery. One of the cashiers told me she and Allessandra left on a cross-country trip. I came to see if they took Jack with them."

Barb bent over and dabbed the drool from Jack's chin with a diaper. She leaned back, glanced up at the ceiling and blew out a puff of air. "Annie, I never told you how sorry I was about the way Allessi behaved, taking Jack away from you like that. I thought all along giving her baby up for adoption was the best thing, and I totally supported her original decision."

Barb reached for a bright red rattle off the table, waited a few seconds for Jack to grasp it and smiled at him.

"But after she had this little guy, she got this bee in her bonnet, you know? She convinced herself she could give Jack the love and attention she saw you give Rafe, and no one was going to change her mind.

"Then she turned eighteen, got the inheritance from her parents, and she thought that would help support both of them. I told her she'd still have to get a part-time job if she wanted the money to last over the next eighteen years until Jack grows up."

"That's good advice."

She nodded. "I thought so, too. She asked me how I'd feel if she and the baby lived here, but Nate and I are planning to buy one of those big RV's, sell this house, and travel around the States. Stacey and Allessi could get an apartment together, but Stacey doesn't want to live with a baby."

Jack dropped the rattle and Barb bent down, picked it up and put it in her breast pocket. "Plus, they'd always talked about going cross-country after they graduated from high school and when Allessi got pregnant Stacey kept hounding her to put the baby up for adoption so they could get out of Brandiss."

"Well," Annie said, "it seems they're living their dream regardless of whether Allessandra has a baby or not. Here you are playing babysitter. It's too bad they're both going to miss out on finishing high school with their friends though."

"But things have changed," Barb interjected.

Annie frowned. "What do you mean?

Barb held up a finger and stood. "One second. Let me wash this off."

Water ran in the kitchen. Barb returned and placed the rattle in Jack's hand again. "That was Allessi on the phone. She wants me to talk to Mr. Mayer."

"What for?"

"This is all so... ," Barb paused, shaking her head. "Before I talk to Mr. Mayer she wants me to ask you whether you're still interested in adopting Jack."

"Is this some sort of sick joke?" Annie whispered.

Barb closed her eyes for a moment, her lips drawn together in a straight line. "Of course not." She massaged her temples with her fingertips. "I swear that girl makes my head spin. I would never have agreed to talk to you about this except this time I believe she's serious. She wants me to ask Mr. Mayer if she can legally waive the waiting period and have you adopt Jack now. Of course, I wasn't expecting you to come to this house, ever. But now that you're here... "

Annie's mind raced in a million directions. What would Prescott think about adopting Jack? More importantly, what about Rafe? All three of them still felt burned from the first fiasco with Allessandra. Annie didn't want to go through that again.

Annie opened her mouth, too afraid to believe this was happening and, at the same time, hoping beyond measure it was true. "Why in God's name would I believe Allessandra is serious this time?"

Barb glanced down for a second, then looked up at Annie, her eyes glassy. A tear escaped down her cheek and she quickly swiped it away with her thumb. "I was so angry... and embarrassed... and humiliated when Allessi took Jack away from you, Annie. We had a huge fight before she went back to talk with the attorney.

"So when she started up again about changing her mind the second time, I told her if she screwed this up, I didn't want to ever see her face again and she had to move out of my house. Stacey agreed with me, too. She told her she'd find someone else to travel with if she thought for one second Allessi wasn't a hundred percent sure about this, this time. Stacey and I aren't going to sit back and let her mess around with your and Rafe's lives again."

"Do you believe her?" Annie asked, her thoughts a jumble of past memories and present hopes.

Barb nodded and gave Annie a small smile. "Yes, I do. When we discussed this before the girls left on their trip, Allessi admitted she'd been totally irresponsible and immature. Personally, I think her decision to take Jack back had something to do with postpartum depression.

"After they decided to go on this trip, she asked if she could leave Jack with me. She wants to prove she's serious about her decision. She said goodbye to him before she left. She wants everything settled while she's away. They don't have any set plans for when they'll return, and she insists she's not changing her mind."

Annie shook her head. "I can't give you an answer right now, Barb. I have to talk to Rafe and Prescott."

Barb gently lifted Jack from Annie's lap, where he lay clasping Annie's thumb in his tiny fist. "I understand. And I'm sorry it took me this long to tell you how sorry I am about what happened."

Annie stood up.

"I know this is a lot to deal with," Barb said, "but if it helps any, I know Allessi pretty well and it's as though she's had a revelation. She knows she didn't handle things well back in May. Now she's doing her best to set it right. I have to keep reminding myself she's a teenager. Hell, she can't face you even now. She thinks you hate her for what she did."

"I don't hate her, Barb. Go ahead and call Mr. Mayer. Then we'll have the information we need concerning the legalities of her new decision." Barb followed Annie to the front door where Annie turned toward her. "What would she do if I said no?"

"Honestly, Annie, she doesn't believe that'll happen. And neither do I. But if you decide against this, Mr. Mayer will handle finding someone to adopt Jack."

Annie stepped out onto the porch, and Barb held the door open.

"I'll call you as soon as I talk to the attorney," Barb said.

Annie turned back around. "I love Jack with all my heart, Barb. But I have to think of my son."

The screen door closed. Through it Annie heard Barb talking to Jack in a low sing-song tone, just as she had when he was hers.

CHAPTER TWENTY-SEVEN

Annie drove home in a daze. She might actually get her baby back, and a joyful note rang in her heart. She zoomed into the driveway at the side of the house and jumped out of the car.

Prescott came around the corner at the same time. "Where's the fire, Annie? You better slow down. Brandiss is a small town. The sheriff is likely to arrest you for speeding."

She grabbed onto his sleeve and tugged. "You're not going to believe what just happened. My God, she's changed her mind, Pres."

He frowned. "Who changed their mind? I thought you went to the supermarket? Did they have an unbelievable sale on paper towels or something?"

"No." She shook her head and took a deep breath. "I was at the supermarket, and Stacey wasn't working at the bakery. She's always there and I usually wave to her. So I asked the checker if he knew where she was. He said she left to go on a cross-country trip with Allessandra. When I asked him if they'd taken Jack with them, he said he didn't know."

His eyebrows shot up. "She took the baby on a trip?"

Annie grasped his arm and shook her head. "No. Wait. I'm trying to tell you. I went to Barb's house and Jack was there."

"Allessandra left Jack with Barb?"

She nodded. "When I got to Barb's house, she told me Allessandra's changed her mind. Allessandra wants to know if I'll adopt Jack."

The expression on his face gave away nothing. "You're telling me that girl has totally reversed her decision? Again?"

"That's exactly what I'm telling you. Barb's going to call me after she talks to Mr. Mayer to see whether Allessandra can waive the legal waiting period and give the baby to me right away."

Prescott took her by the shoulders and stared in her eyes. "Don't do this. Don't get your hopes up again."

Tears rimmed Annie's eyes, but she refused to cry unhappy tears. Not now. Not when the possibility of getting Jack seemed so real. "I know I shouldn't get my hopes up, Pres. But from everything Barb told me, Allessandra realizes how irresponsibly she acted and she knows she can't take care of a baby at her age." Annie's pulse pounded in her ears.

Prescott took hold of her hands. "What did you tell Barb?"

She turned, grabbed a few grocery bags and placed them in Prescott's arms. "Let's put these away." She reached in to get the last bag. "I told her I had to talk to Rafe. And with you, of course. Barb will probably call me tonight if she gets in touch with Mr. Mayer."

Annie rushed into the kitchen, Prescott trailing behind her. While putting the groceries away, she said, "I know it's completely insane to get excited about this. But Barb said Allessandra decided this a while ago. And if I don't do this, Mr. Mayer will handle the adoption and find someone else. Either way, Allessandra's not keeping Jack."

He pulled her in for a hug. "You're right about one thing, Annie. It's insane to get psyched about this. I don't want you to get hurt again. How long has it been since she took Jack away from you?"

She stepped back. "It's not over 'til it's over, Prescott. If Mr. Mayer and Allessandra work this out somehow, I'm signing those papers, dammit." Tears dripped down her cheeks. "I want him back. Don't you feel the same way?"

He leaned down and kissed her softly. "Of course I want him back. I loved him, too. Correct that. I still love him. And naturally you want him back. But if Allessandra's screwing around with you, I swear I'll kill her with my bare hands."

She laid her head on his chest and wrapped her arms around him. "I know she's young. And I know she changed her mind once. And she could do it again." She edged away from him. "Let's just wait for Barb to call. Then we'll know what's really going on, okay?"

"What about Rafe?" Worry dripped from his every word.

"I'm sure as hell not going to say anything to him right now. It killed me to see him so broken up the first time. If it happened again, he'd be beyond consoling."

Prescott's face was etched with concern. "You'd be devastated too, Annie. And that wouldn't be good for you, or our baby. We've got to think about this objectively, Honey. You can think positively but don't believe it's gonna happen until it does, all right?"

She embraced him again and clung to him for support. He was her rock in bad times, as well as the good ones. "You're right. We should wait until the papers are in my hands, with Allessandra's signature plastered all over them, before we tell Rafe a thing."

That night, while Rafe played with his Guitar Hero, the phone rang. Prescott and Annie sat in the kitchen and she picked up the cordless phone. It was Barb.

"I talked to Mr. Mayer. He said that in California, if the birth mother is at least eighteen years old, she can legally waive the waiting period."

Annie tried not to get excited. "Allessandra already turned eighteen," she replied in a monotone.

"Yeah. That's when she made this decision."

Annie closed her eyes. She couldn't believe this was happening.

"There are definitely advantages to turning eighteen, Annie," Barb said. She drew in a breath. "Have you decided what you want to do?"

"If I want to adopt Jack, what happens now? Legally, that is."

"Allessandra would have to sign certain legal documents. Mr. Mayer would draw them up and fax them to her attorney in New Mexico."

"New Mexico?"

"You're not going to believe this. Stacey and Allessandra took a map and spun a coin on top of it. They said they'd drive to wherever the coin landed."

Annie didn't know what to say. In her opinion it was more proof of Allessandra's immaturity. Perhaps Allessandra would decide she didn't like being on the road every day and want to come back to Brandiss, pick up where she left off, return to being a mom and want Jack again.

Annie's thoughts were interrupted with, "Annie? You there?"

"Sorry, Barb, I was just thinking, what if she changes her mind again and comes back from her trip and wants Jack?"

"If you want to do this, Mr. Mayer will explain everything to you in detail, Annie. He told me if you decide to adopt Jack, you'll sign legal papers, work out the financial end of things, Allessandra will sign certain documents, and he'll file the papers in court. After that she'll have no legal grounds for taking Jack back. That's it."

Annie held the phone so tightly, her fingernails dug into her palm. "I'll call Mr. Mayer tomorrow morning and talk with him first. But thank you, Barb. I appreciate everything you've done."

"Don't thank me, Annie. Between you and me, Jack will have a much better life with you. I've always believed that."

Annie placed the phone on the counter and turned to Prescott. The first tear escaped down her cheek.

"What did she say?"

She shook her head, unable to talk.

"You're going to talk with Mr. Mayer in the morning, right?"

She nodded. "Barb said Allessandra can waive the waiting period which would allow me to adopt Jack immediately. She said it's all legal, but I want to hear it from Mr. Mayer."

He pulled her onto his lap. "That's a very smart way to handle it. I don't want to sound like a broken record, but just be cautious. Wait until all the i's are dotted and the t's are crossed, before you put your whole heart into this."

She lifted one leg over and straddled him, their faces inches apart. She wrapped her arms around his neck. "I know you're right. I keep telling myself to slow down. Everything's happening too fast. Intellectually, I know Jack won't be mine until all the papers are signed, but emotionally, it's difficult for me not to jump up and dance."

He placed his hands along her waist and pulled her in closer, lightly nibbling her neck, before he engaged her lips in a slow kiss. She responded instantly, hormones raging. Both of them wanted a more active sex life but she'd only just begun feeling better and they rarely had time alone.

Prescott's arousal blossomed as Annie moved her pelvis over the fly of his jeans. His hands roved under her shirt, fingers squeezing her nipples. Annie's body shivered with desire. She ground her hips against the bulge beneath her lower body and sucked gently on his bottom lip.

They were playing a game they couldn't finish, knowing Rafe

was in the other room. She pushed against his chest with both hands and pulled away from his embrace. "This is an excellent way to make me forget my worries, you know. If we could do this all day I would never be concerned about anything."

He continued massaging her breasts beneath her shirt and covered her mouth with a thorough kiss. "I don't enjoy seeing you so upset. I wanted to distract you." His laugh was low and husky.

She grinned. "Thanks for trying, but we'll have to plan a time to continue this at a later date."

"Where's your calendar?" he asked seriously and pulled his hands out from underneath her shirt.

She leaned in and gave him her version of a final kiss, and then whispered, "Get out of here while you can or I won't be able to keep my hands off you."

He stood up to leave and rearranged his clothes before walking out the front door.

CHAPTER TWENTY-EIGHT

When Annie called Mr. Mayer the next morning, he reiterated what Barb had told her. He still had the file in his office dealing with Annie's first attempt to adopt Jack, the home study had already been completed, and only a short time had passed since Allessandra took Jack back, so all the paperwork was considered legally current. This would allow Mr. Mayer to draw up the legal documents, ready for Annie's signature immediately.

After listening to his lengthy explanation, she said, "And what if she changes her mind again, Mr. Mayer? Obviously, I don't want to go through what happened last time."

"I understand. However, the fact this is California and she's turned eighteen, she can waive the waiting period. Which completely changes the nature of the adoption. Once I've filed the papers in court, they're legally binding. Jack becomes your son."

"When would you file the papers?"

"If you decide to do this, Mrs. Davidson, I could get on the docket the same day Allessandra signs the final adoption papers."

Annie turned toward Prescott who was sitting beside her at the kitchen table. She had the phone on speaker so he was able to listen to the entire conversation. Prescott smiled at her and squeezed her hand.

"I could be there this morning," she said.

"How about ten-thirty?"

"See you then." She set the phone down and closed her eyes.

"Breathe, Annie," Prescott whispered.

"Is this really happening?"

"I guess it is."

She opened her eyes. "Will you come with me?"

"Of course I'll come with you. Seeing you sign those documents will be one of the highlights of my life."

"Mine, too." She jumped up. "I better get ready." She raced upstairs to change clothes. They only had an hour-and-a-half before Annie's appointment.

The drive seemed to take forever. When they finally arrived at the lawyer's office, Annie was so nervous she could hardly hold the pen steady. Now Allessandra had to sign the same documents and set a date for Annie to pick up Jack. They were almost there.

They drove back to Brandiss and picked up Rafe from school. They agreed not to discuss anything about Jack's adoption, but it was very difficult to pretend it was just another day. However, it was understood they were doing it for Rafe's sake.

Mr. Mayer phoned early the next morning. He faxed Allessandra the papers, she signed them and faxed them back to his office. He'd file them in court at ten a.m. that same day and then phone Annie immediately afterward so she could pick up Jack.

Annie phoned Barb, who was waiting for her call. Barb told her she'd be home all day. Annie took a shower, put on her make-up, blow-dried her hair and tried not to think about the minutes ticking away.

Despite Mr. Mayer's reassurance, Annie still feared Allessandra would change her mind at the last moment. Prescott and Annie passed the remaining time in the nursery, arranging furniture and making sure the room was ready for the baby. By the time ten o'clock rolled around, Annie's heart was pounding so hard she had to sit down.

The phone rang at ten-twenty-five.

"Congratulations." The always serious Mr. Mayer actually sounded as if he were happy.

"Thank you," Annie said, tears coursing down her cheeks.

"You can pick up your baby," he continued. "I'll send you copies of the final documents."

Prescott pulled her in for a hug and all the tension and fear began to slowly subside from her mind and body.

"Ready to go?" he said.

She grinned. "Are you kidding me?" She swiped at her wet face, grabbed her purse and Prescott took hold of her hand as they rushed out the door to the truck. When they pulled up to Barb's house, Barb pushed open the front door, holding Jack in her arms.

Annie glanced over at Prescott as he pulled the key out of the ignition. "I can't believe this is happening," she whispered.

He gave her a quick kiss and squeezed her hand. "Believe it." He jumped out of the truck and came over to her side to help her down. Her legs felt too shaky to walk and she needed him by her side.

Time slowed to a crawl. Barb stood on the porch but it took forever for Annie to walk there. Each step felt as though she was moving through thick mud.

Prescott stopped at the bottom of the stairs and pulled his hand out of her grasp. When Annie turned toward him, he whispered, "Go get your son, Annie."

A smile flickered across her lips. He was giving her this moment, this unique blip in time, to experience solely with Jack, to remember forever as an unbelievable gift.

Barb held Jack out to Annie, like the present he truly was, and Annie took him in her arms, tears clouding her eyes. Jack's tiny face blurred as Annie stared down at him.

Barb and Prescott exchanged friendly words but they sounded miles away. Jack smiled at Annie. Maybe he hadn't forgotten who she was. He'd always held a place in Annie's heart, waiting for his return, and today he'd come back to her.

Barb patted Annie on the back then walked inside the house.

"Let's go, you two," Prescott said softly.

Annie nodded, and they returned to the truck. She held Jack on her lap then looked at Prescott over the top of Jack's tiny head... and grinned.

"Are you ever going to let go of him?" he teased.

She gazed down at Jack's chubby face. "He's ours now." She paused. Words couldn't describe the awesomeness. "I have him back." Tears slipped down her cheeks as reality sank in.

Prescott put his arm around her shoulders and kissed her forehead then leaned toward Jack. "Hey, little guy. This is your Mommy." Prescott laid his huge palm on the top of Jack's head. "We'll have a houseful soon, huh? Rafe, Jack, and our new baby."

Amazing. This little boy was her son again. "Let's go home."

"Good idea. He can sleep in his crib with all the toys I bought him. Remember how Rafe used to line them up along the sides while Jack watched that thingee go around that hung over the crib?"

Annie laughed. "It's called a mobile, silly. And of course I remember. We'd better go. It's a short day at school today. A teacher's conference or something. We don't have much time before we have to pick up Rafe."

He started the engine, and they drove the few blocks home. "How about I stay home with Jack while you pick up Rafe from school? You'll have to prepare him for this, Annie."

"I know. It'll be such a shock. But he'll be so excited, Pres."

When one o'clock rolled around, Annie drove to the school. Rafe opened the door of the car, jumped in, and turned toward her. "Can we go get ice cream?"

She was anxious to have their conversation so Rafe could see Jack, but she knew she had to take the time to explain this surprising news to him, and give him at least a few minutes to digest it.

"Sure. Maxwell's Ice Cream Parlor?"

He nodded, smiling. "Double chocolate chip on a sugar cone."

She grinned, her heart full. She knew he'd be so excited once she told him about Jack.

Annie drove the few blocks to Maxwell's on Main Street where they stood in line to order. After getting their cones, they stepped outside and sat at one of the glass-topped tables that lined the sidewalk in front of the parlor.

Rafe worked his tongue round and round the edge of the cone.

"I have some good news, Honey. About Jack."

He glanced at her, his tongue still sticking out, covered with ice cream. He sat back in his chair and swallowed, wiped his mouth with the back of his hand. "What?"

"Allessandra has decided she isn't the best mother for Jack. She asked if we still wanted to adopt him. I've already signed all the papers and Jack is ours now. She can't take him away from us this time, Rafe. That's the law. He's your baby brother, forever."

She'd hoped for shouts of joy, but Rafe wasn't smiling. He looked confused.

"Jack's gonna live with us? Allessandra can't take him back?"

She leaned over and placed a hand on his shoulder. "Honey, she can't take him away from us ever. He's your brother, for always. I promise."

He stared at her, unblinking. Ice cream dripped onto his hand, and she grabbed several napkins. "Here Honey, take these. You okay?"

He blinked a few times, glanced down at his cone, and back up at her. "When can I see him?"

She smiled. "He's at home right now with Prescott. We picked him up at Barb's house this morning. Do you want to finish your ice cream cone before we head home?"

He stood up quickly. The chair wobbled on the concrete. "No." He rushed over to the garbage can and dumped his cone and napkins in the trash. "I'm ready."

She threw her cone away too. They ran over to the car and were home in minutes. She pulled into the driveway and was taking the key out of the ignition when Rafe bolted for the front door. She caught up with him as he stood in the foyer, frowning.

"He's upstairs in the crib," she said and closed the front door.

Rafe ran up the stairs. As Annie reached the top landing, Rafe opened the nursery door, his hand on the knob, twisting it slowly. He hesitated just a second before he pushed it open and walked toward the crib on the far side of the room near the window.

Annie stood at the doorway, Prescott behind her. He wrapped his arms around her waist and watched the scene play out over her shoulder. Rafe reached through the bars of the crib and touched Jack's little fingers, tears rolling down his face.

But he was smiling. And so were they.

CHAPTER TWENTY-NINE

By August the judge granted Prescott the service of publication. It would be another six weeks before he went back to court to find out whether the judge would agree to the divorce. He moved the majority of his things to Ivy Place and slept there most nights, and planned to lease out his house. His antique furniture complimented Annie's perfectly. Jack and Annie quickly got back into a comfortable routine and the baby was sleeping through the night.

Every evening after dinner, Prescott, Rafe, and Annie watched television or played games while Jack sat in his baby seat, gurgling and smiling at all the attention. A good majority of time Annie spent caring for the baby, and Rafe soon became bored just hanging around the house all day. So Annie enrolled him in a basketball clinic for two weeks.

Jack was taking a nap and Annie was picking up around the house, enjoying the sounds of the birds chirping in the trees, the wind rustling through the willows, when the distinct rumble of Prescott's truck broke the silence. He must have forgotten something he needed for work.

His footsteps echoed through the screen door as he climbed the stairs, pulled the door open, and walked into the front room. She'd never seen his face that way, pulled taut over his cheekbones. He greeted her with a terse, "Hi," and she could tell something wasn't right.

"What're you doing home?"

Without a word, he sat on the couch and patted the cushion next to him.

She sat beside him and whispered, "What's wrong? Rafe's all right, isn't he? No one contacted you from the basketball clinic, did they?"

"No, Annie. It's nothing like that." He paused.

"You're scaring me. What's going on?"

He clasped her hands in his and looked into her eyes. "The sheriff's office called me. Patti and Dylan are in Santa Barbara."

"Oh my God." What would this mean for Prescott? What would it mean for her and for Rafe and Jack, for their unborn child? "Where have they been?"

"The sheriff told me she walked into the station and turned herself in. He didn't say much, but I guess she asked to see me. He said I should get there as soon as possible." He let out a sigh. "It's been almost three years."

"So you're driving to Santa Barbara? Now?" After the words left her mouth, she knew how silly she sounded.

He clasped her shoulders and looked her straight in the eyes. "I need to see Patti, face to face. I want her to tell me why she took my son away from me."

She stared at her hands, folded in her lap. "She must have been pretty messed up to kidnap him."

"I know. I'm anxious to find out the specifics."

Fear filled Annie's mind and body. Fear he'd go back to Patti, fear he'd leave her all alone with Rafe and Jack after they'd formed their rather unconventional family bond, fear they'd lose another person whom they loved dearly.

Maybe Prescott would want to get back together with Patti. He still loved her. Family was extremely important to him. Annie envisioned Prescott forgiving Patti, taking her back, continuing their life together.

Annie shook so badly, her knees knocked together. "You should go," she said, trying her best not to cry in front of him.

He covered her hands with his. "You're shaking, Annie."

She felt a tear escape down her cheek. "I love you, Prescott."

He hugged her tightly. "And I love you." His expression turned serious. "I have to do this. But I'm coming back. I promise."

She nodded, not daring to open her mouth. If she did, she knew the sob she was holding back would escape her lips.

He gave Annie a tender kiss before he walked out the door.

That kiss might be their last. They hugged. Their final goodbye? They may have just shared their last moment together.

Annie didn't know how this was going to turn out, but she had to stay calm for the baby growing inside her. She had to keep her emotions in check until she knew what was really going on. If she fell apart, it would be bad for Jack, and Rafe as well. She had to take care of her children, no matter what happened.

Annie picked Rafe up from school and said nothing about Prescott. Rafe played on the swing set in the back yard. Jack entertained himself in his bouncy seat. She fixed dinner then watched a Disney movie with Rafe before she walked him upstairs and put him to bed.

By then it was nine-thirty and Prescott hadn't phoned. Annie presumed it might take hours. He needed to deal with the sheriff's office, and the FBI was probably involved, and all this was taking place in Santa Barbara.

Prescott and Patti would have a lot to talk about after spending three years apart. Annie imagined different scenarios of what could be happening between them, from rage and anger, to loving embraces and words of "I've missed you." It was killing her, not knowing, but she couldn't do anything about it. Life was, once again, out of her control.

She tried to sleep that night and managed to drift off for little spurts at a time. The baby kicked so much, it felt like she or he was trying to escape. Her emotional state wasn't doing her or her child any good.

She tried deep breathing exercises to keep focused and less stressed. When she glanced at the clock, for what seemed like the millionth time, it was six a.m. Time to get up.

When she walked into the kitchen, her cell phone, which she'd left on the counter, was making its little chirping noise. If Prescott phoned he would have called the landline so Annie guessed she must have received a text message. Flipping it open, it flashed "Text from Prescott" on the screen. She pressed the "View Now" button: "Talked to Patti. Saw Dylan. In touch soon."

Annie's future was in the making at this moment. She could only surmise he and Patti had reached some sort of understanding. Maybe they'd go away together for a few days, try to see whether they could make it work again.

Her heart was breaking. She felt physically ill, imagining Prescott in Patti's arms, kissing her, making love to her. She pictured him picking up Dylan, laughing, Patti watching, enjoying themselves again as a family. She wanted to crawl back into bed and cry.

She felt as bad as the day she dropped Jack off at the attorney's office. She couldn't do this again. She wouldn't do this again. But what was the alternative?

She didn't hear from Prescott all that long, long day. And there was no phone call in the middle of the night, no text message on her cell. Nothing. He'd left to see Patti and Dylan two days ago. She was a complete wreck. She forced herself to eat breakfast, lunch, and dinner, solely for the baby.

She tried to keep to a normal routine for Rafe and Jack, and not let on that anything was awry. But, by that evening, she was going crazy with worry, mulling over the same scenario again and again.

She put the two kids to bed a little early and sat down to write a letter to Prescott, telling him she understood he had to do what was right by Patti and Dylan.

She had to do something.

She planned to drive to his house and put the note on his front door. She placed the tip of her pen on the piece of stationary and a familiar sound sliced through her reverie—the rumble of Prescott's truck. Her stomach clenched, her mouth went dry, a whooshing sound reverberated inside her head.

She'd know her future in moments and she wanted to run out the back door. She didn't want to face this. She was so afraid of hearing what he'd tell her. Her body shook involuntarily. She was more afraid than she'd ever been in her life. Fight or flight? But there was nowhere to go.

He approached the front door and Annie walked over to open it. He immediately took her in his arms and held her.

He pulled back slightly. "I love you, Annie," he whispered before he kissed her. He took her hand and led her over to the couch. "Can we talk?"

Annie's throat constricted, lips unable to move.

"It was so unreal," he began, pulling her onto the couch. "I walked into the sheriff's station and Patti was sitting in one of those interrogation rooms. She appeared so much older, like she'd aged ten years since I'd seen her. She just sat there, staring down at the table before she mumbled that she needed to explain what happened."

He took both Annie's hands in his. "Annie, I swear it was like seeing a stranger. Her eyes were lifeless, her hair hadn't been washed in days. It was awful. She asked me not to say anything and just let her explain first." He drew a shuddering breath and gazed out the window.

Were he and Annie finished? Would Annie have to wish him well on his reunion with his wife?

She couldn't wait any longer. "What is it, Pres?"

His gaze seemed riveted on something outside the window. "She said she never wanted to marry me in the first place. That I forced her to get married after she got pregnant with Dylan." His eyebrows drew down in a tight vee. Was he hurt? Sad? Annie wasn't sure yet.

His eyes were rimmed with unshed tears. "She's right. At first she was against getting married, but I convinced her it was a good idea. And she seemed okay with it. I thought we were in love. She was going to have our baby." He paused. "After she gave birth to Dylan, I guess she freaked out, felt like she'd gotten herself into a situation she never wanted in the first place, being tied down to one man forever."

He drew in a deep breath and let it out slowly. "After a few months, she said she had to get out but she knew I'd try to talk her out of it. Which is true. So she took Dylan, got on a bus, paid cash for everything, made a new life for herself in New York, worked for money under the table. She met some artist guy, fell in love, moved in with him, and they traveled around the country to craft fairs, selling their art work."

"But what about Dylan?"

"Her boyfriend's sister took care of him while they were on the road. Which was often. She finally realized the life she wanted wasn't exactly conducive to having a child."

"So now what? She wants you to babysit him while she travels around with her lover?"

He hugged her and drew back. "No." He shook his head. "I told her I want a divorce. And full custody of Dylan."

Annie held her breath and the crack in her heart began to slowly close. "What did she say?"

He smiled. "I won't press charges for kidnapping, she'll agree to my getting full custody of Dylan, and we're getting a divorce."

Annie smiled for the first time. "This is unbelievable."

"I paid for her to stay in a hotel in Santa Barbara for a few days, after I posted her bail. I talked to Mr. Mayer, and Patti and I are meeting with a partner in his firm tomorrow, to go over the legal documents concerning the divorce and custody."

"I'm so happy for you."

"What's wrong, Annie?"

"Maybe you need some time with Dylan to get acquainted. He doesn't even know who you are, Prescott."

"You, Rafe and Jack are my family now. I need to be with you."

Tears filled her eyes. "You have your son back."

He wrapped her in his arms and whispered, "When this is all over, we can get married, Annie. No more waiting." He gave her a stern look. "I'm happy to have my son back, but my life won't be complete until I have you and Rafe and Jack, until we're all a family." He brushed the tears from her cheeks. "You'll still marry me?"

Annie responded with equal ardor, hugging him tightly. She needed reassurance that he still wanted her as much as she wanted him.

He pulled back. "You haven't answered my question."

Annie let out a deep, grateful sigh and answered, "Yes, I'll still marry you."

CHAPTER THIRTY

The following day, Prescott and Patti met with Mr. Mayer's partner, Shelby Carrington. Annie was anxious for him to come back with all the information that would give them a sense of closure.

It wasn't until nine that evening that Prescott called Annie from his cell phone. "Everything went well. Ms. Carrington is as thorough as Mr. Mayer. I was impressed."

Annie let out a sigh. "What a relief. Patti signed all the papers? Do you have Dylan with you?"

He laughed. "He's right here, safe and sound. Our divorce won't be final for several months, but I have custody of him anyway. He's asleep in the back seat. Poor guy's exhausted."

"I bet he is. How'd everything go? You know, between Patti and Dylan?"

"Taking him from Patti was kind of weird. He's almost four, he doesn't remember me, and he knows something's not right. It's not normal to just give your kid over to a stranger and expect him to be okay with it. But he didn't even cry, Annie. Sounds like he spent a lot of time with babysitters while Patti and her boyfriend traveled around, so maybe he doesn't think it's odd to be dropped off with somebody he doesn't know."

"I feel sorry for him. And for you, too, Pres. But it's Patti's fault. It didn't have to be this way."

He sighed. "I would have fought against us getting a divorce, but that's no excuse for kidnapping my son. I just wanted to let you know I'm on my way back. I should be there in about thirty minutes. Are Rafe and Jack asleep?"

"I just put them to bed. Dylan can sleep in the extra bed in Jack's room."

It wasn't long before he pulled up in front of the house. Annie rushed to open the door. Dylan lay asleep in his arms.

"Oh my God, he's your clone. I bet you looked just like this when you were a little boy." She kissed Dylan's dark curly hair, breathing in his scent, like lead pencils and outdoors. "I'm already in love with him."

Prescott's eyes were glassy. "Isn't he gorgeous, Annie? How could Patti give him up?"

Annie glanced at Dylan again, his features so serene in dreamland. "That's all behind you now. Don't even think about it ever again. Tomorrow's a new day and we'll have our family all together. It'll be so fun when Rafe and Jack meet him."

"What a houseful, eh? Did you ever think you'd have three kids and another on the way?"

She laughed quietly. "No. But that doesn't mean I don't love it." She stood on her tiptoes and kissed Prescott gently. "As long as we're together, everything will be fine."

"Let's put D to bed. He's had a long day."

"You called him 'D'."

"That's what I used to call him when he was a baby. My little D. D."

They brought him upstairs to Jack's room. Annie helped Prescott remove Dylan's shirt and shoes and tuck him in bed before they quietly made their way downstairs. Prescott was exhausted and instantly fell asleep with his head on her shoulder.

Annie coaxed him awake and they headed back upstairs, where they made love quietly and slowly. She was drained from the past few days of emotional turmoil, but needed to feel the passion that was always there between them. Her next recollection was the sun shining in her eyes and Jack whimpering in the nursery.

After Rafe woke up, both Prescott and Annie sat with him while he ate his Captain Crunch.

"Hey, buddy," Prescott said. "I need to talk to you about something."

Rafe nodded his head as he slurped the cereal from a spoon.

"Remember I told you about my wife, Patti, and my son, Dylan?"

"Uh-huh. They maybe were kidnapped, but the police can't find them, right?"

"Patti came back with Dylan the other night. They're alive."

Rafe held his spoon half-way to his mouth. "Where are they?"

"Patti arrived in Santa Barbara. I met with her and saw Dylan at the same time."

Rafe glanced at Annie, and then back at Prescott. "Are you gonna leave us?"

Prescott shook his head and smiled. "No, I'm not going anywhere, Rafe. Patti and I are getting a divorce. When she left me and took Dylan three years ago, she was very unhappy. She doesn't want to be married. She wants to travel."

"Kinda like Allessandra, right? She wants to travel, too. That's why she gave Jack back to me and Mom."

Prescott grinned. His eyes told her how much he adored her son. "Right, kind of like Allessandra. But while Patti was traveling someone else took care of Dylan and that's not the sort of life Patti wanted for our son. Dylan will be living with me from now on."

Rafe's eyebrows dipped down. "You mean he's gonna live here with us?"

"Is that alright with you? He's almost four and a good little kid. He'll be like your baby brother."

Rafe stared at Prescott, a frown on his face. "I already have a brother."

Prescott looked at Annie with a blank expression. This was something Annie needed to handle. Rafe was her son, and it was Annie's responsibility to try and make this right.

"Prescott and Patti will be getting a divorce. As soon as that happens he and I want to get married. Dylan will legally be your baby brother. We'll be a family just like we are now. But a bigger family. Dylan's closer to your age than Jack, and you could play together."

His eyes flashed, lips set in a straight line. "So now I'll have two brothers, and another sister or brother who's gonna be born in December. It used to be just you and me."

Prescott and Annie exchanged worried glances. It was true. Their family had grown by leaps and bounds in a few short months.

Rafe dropped his spoon in his bowl, splashing milk on the table. "It isn't fair," he yelled and stood up, his chair crashed to the floor.

Annie's mouth dropped open. She'd never seen him so mad. He'd become much more adept at dealing with life's sudden tilts and turns, but perhaps this was just too much for such a young boy to handle.

He ran out of the kitchen and bounded up the stairs, followed by the slam of his bedroom door.

Prescott turned to follow him, and Annie placed her hand on his forearm. "Wait. Let me talk to him first, see how it goes. Depending on what he says, maybe you and he can talk afterward, okay?"

Prescott kissed her lightly on the lips. "I'll wait here."

Annie walked up the stairs and knocked on Rafe's bedroom door. He didn't answer but she was sure he knew who was on the other side, so she turned the handle and stepped inside. He lay face down on the bed, his little head pressed into the pillow.

Annie sat on the side of the bed, placed her hand on his head and stroked the silky strands of his hair. "I understand what's bothering you, Honey."

He threw the pillow aside and sat up, eyes red and swollen, his face splotchy from crying. "It used to be just you and me."

"I know."

He seemed to look right through her. "We adopted Jack and you had to take care of him." He paused, his lower lip quivered with emotion. "But Prescott was always around. We played baseball and he took me to the park." Tears coursed down his smooth cheeks and fell onto the bedspread.

"So what's making you so sad?"

"Now Dylan will be here." He stared at his hands and twisted the edge of the sheet. "Now no one will play with me. You'll be too busy with Jack and Prescott'll have Dylan." He threw himself back on the bed, grabbed the pillow and sobbed into it.

Annie's heart squeezed. She felt the pain emanating from her young son, and all she wanted was to make it go away. He'd been the center of her life since he was born and nothing would change that. He'd endured more than enough sorrow in his young life. Maybe it had been too much for a child his age. But she was determined to fix this, make it right.

"Rafe, that's not what's going to happen."

"How do you know?" he said, his voice hardly audible through the down pillow covering his face.

"Sit up, baby, so we can talk."

Slowly, he sat up. She placed her fingertips under his chin and moved his head, forcing him to look at her straight-on.

"Every morning I'm going to take you to school, like I always do. Every afternoon I'm going to pick you up, like I always do. I'll help you with your homework after school like always. After that, you and Prescott will play ball or go to the park like you usually do. We'll have dinner together like we always do, and play games or watch a movie. You're not going to be alone. Ever. I'll make sure of that.

"And maybe you and I can have one day a week, or on the weekend, and just the two of us will do something together. And if you want, Prescott will do the same thing. You will not be alone, Honey. Our family is just getting bigger, that's all."

He shook his head. "But he's got Dylan now. His real son."

She pulled him closer to her side and hugged him tightly. "Yes, Dylan is Prescott's son, but he loves you, Rafe. And he's not going to replace you with Dylan. He won't do that."

He shrugged his small shoulders. "How do you know?"

"Why don't I let him talk to you about this?" She glanced down at him. He looked so forlorn and sad. "Wait right here, okay?" She rushed down the stairs.

Prescott was still in the kitchen, sitting at the table drinking a cup of coffee.

"Where's Jack?" she said.

"I just put him down for a nap. Dylan's still asleep. He's had a rough week. He must be exhausted. How's Rafe?"

Annie sat in the chair next to him. "He thinks he's going to be left out because you'll have Dylan so you won't play with him anymore. And I'll be busy with Jack and the new baby. I told him I'd still be dropping him off at school, picking him up, helping him with his homework, and maybe we'll have a special day together each week. I said you loved him and nothing would change your relationship with him. But he doesn't believe me."

"Could I talk with him?"

She nodded.

"I'd like to explain to him how much I love him. And I think he and Dylan will eventually have a good time together. It might take a while to adjust, but I really believe we've got some terrific kids, Annie."

She leaned over and laid a chaste kiss on his lips. "Me, too. Why don't you go? He's waiting."

His heavy footsteps thumped up the stairs. The bedroom door closed behind him. She hoped Rafe would believe them, but she also knew they'd have to prove to him their words were more than wishes. And she was determined to show him she wasn't trying to make him feel better with empty promises.

Annie busied herself cleaning up the kitchen table and after what seemed like forever, Rafe's voice came toward the kitchen.

"Feeling better?" she asked.

Prescott nodded. "Rafe and I have plans to go to the next Dodger's game." He looked down at Rafe. "And if he likes that, I told him I'd get season tickets."

Rafe sat at the table next to Annie. "He said if we get season tickets it'll be just him and me going. And we can go to as many games as we want."

Annie smiled and rubbed his back. "That's a great idea. Just the two of you in Los Angeles. What a cool thing to do."

Rafe and Prescott smiled at each other. Annie let out a shaky breath.

"I have to check on Dylan," Prescott said. "We'll be down in a minute."

Rafe twisted a paper napkin round and round between his fingers. She knew he must be nervous and hoped this first encounter would go smoothly.

Several minutes later, Prescott and Dylan entered the kitchen. The boys stared at each other. Dylan hadn't seen his father since he was nine months old and all of them were complete strangers to him.

"Hi," Rafe said, breaking the silence.

Dylan opened his mouth and Prescott nodded at him. "Hi," Dylan whispered.

"How old are you?" Rafe asked.

"Almost four," Dylan said in a small voice.

"So you're three," Rafe countered.

Annie tried to keep a straight face. "When's your birthday, sweetie?"

Dylan raised both hands, fingers splayed. "November ten," he said, speaking a little louder.

Prescott knelt down next to where Dylan was standing. "What's your favorite kind of cake, D?"

Dylan smiled, the first since his arrival. "Peanut butter."

Prescott chuckled. "Peanut butter cake? Never heard of it. I bet Annie could bake one for you though."

Dylan smiled at Annie again.

She knelt on the floor next to Prescott. Her heart went out to this little boy. They'd never know what his life had been like with his mother. But now Patti was free of her responsibility to him and hopefully, they would never hear from her again.

"I'll bake you a peanut butter cake for your fourth birthday, Dylan. And you can help me. You could lick the beaters. Have you ever done that before?"

With a blank expression, he said, "No."

"Rafe and I do that all the time," she said and glanced at Rafe. "In fact, Rafe and I could make you a cake before your birthday and you and Rafe can lick the beaters."

Dylan smiled for the third time.

"Let's all go out in the back yard," Annie said, looking from Dylan to Rafe. "You can get to know each other while you're playing outside."

By the end of the day, the two boys were talking to each other. She considered that a giant step in the right direction. Rafe owned every single Thomas the Tank Engine piece and Dylan had never seen one before. They built an entire train station and neighboring village.

Prescott and Annie watched them interact throughout the afternoon and evening. They were far enough apart in age that Dylan looked up to Rafe for guidance. Prescott and Annie guessed that might defer much of the competition between the two. They could only hope and trust the two of them would eventually bond.

Annie didn't think Rafe had any real issue with Dylan but rather the attention he would lose if Prescott and she weren't diligent about spending time with him as well. But Annie knew Prescott would live up to his promise, taking extra care to continue to pay close attention to her son. And Rafe had always been the center of her universe and that would never change.

Though it was a new world for all of them now, Annie had faith that they'd grow accustomed to the new dynamics of a family of six.

CHAPTER THIRTY-ONE

The past eighteen months had brought unexpected, though ultimately wonderful, changes in Annie's life. Rafe and she moved to Brandiss, adopted Jack, Dylan joined their family, and she was having Prescott's child in December. It had been the roller coaster ride of their lives. Annie looked forward to many quiet months ahead, filled with serene anticipation with their new baby, and Prescott and Annie could legally marry as soon as his divorce was final.

It was September and business had been slow for Prescott since finishing work on their home. He was actively seeking new clients, but there was nothing on the horizon and he'd completed his last project weeks ago.

He came home one day looking pensive. He'd been less talkative lately, and Annie hoped things would be looking up for him soon. He walked into the kitchen and asked if she had a few minutes to talk. Annie followed him into the front room and they sat on the couch.

He leaned his elbows on his knees. "I've been scrounging around everywhere for new clients. I've gone to Santa Barbara, Carpinteria, Sea Cliff, and I can't find any work. The money we have in savings won't last forever, and now with three kids and another on the way we have to think about the kids' future, and our own retirement."

She nodded. "You're right. The money I got from Cam's death won't last forever. I used a big chunk of it to buy this house. I never dreamed one day I'd have four kids. And I want to stay at home with them."

"I have a friend. James Dunsmuir. He and I went to college together and after we graduated he moved back home to the Bay Area. I called him today. He's the structural foreman for the new Bay Bridge span between Oakland and San Francisco. He's looking for an assistant foreman."

"What did you tell him?"

He held up his index finger. "Wait. It gets better. The project will take around seven years. We're talking job security, benefit package, retirement plan, medical, dental, three times the amount I'm making now."

"Where would we live?"

"I don't think either of us wants to live in a big city, Annie. The company has a credit union that assists employees with home loans. He told me to talk it over with you and call him back."

She took his hand. "You're frowning, Pres."

"How would you feel about moving back to the Bay Area?"

She looked down at their clasped hands. "As much as I love this old house, I could live in the Bay Area again. We could buy a house anywhere we want. It's not like we'd be living in Sausalito."

"James and his wife, Kathleen, live in Alameda. Are you familiar with the place?"

"I've been there. Lots of Victorian homes, old Craftsman style houses."

He kissed her and whispered, "Do you want to go for it?"

She nodded.

"You are one fantastic fiancée, Annie."

"I think you're pretty fantastic too, Pres."

He phoned James Dunsmuir that evening. Prescott planned to contact the credit union the next day and they'd search online for homes in Alameda as well. There wasn't much time to get settled into a new home before the baby was born.

Jack and Dylan were taking a nap, and Prescott, Rafe, and Annie were having lunch the next day. Annie nodded at Prescott.

He took a deep breath. "Your mom and I want to talk to you about something, Rafe."

Rafe's eyebrows shot up, his mouth full of peanut butter and jelly sandwich.

"A friend of mine called last night. He has a huge job he wants me to help him with in San Francisco. It would pay me a lot of money. But we'd have to move."

Rafe swallowed the last bit of his sandwich and turned toward Annie. "I don't wanna leave."

"Honey, when you and I moved into this house," she said, "I had no idea Prescott, Jack and Dylan would be living with us. And don't forget we have a new baby on the way. Soon there will be six of us. This house just isn't big enough."

"Why can't we buy another house in Brandiss then?"

"Rafe, if we buy a bigger house it will cost more than this one and that would be very expensive. I can't work outside the home. I have to take care of you, Jack, and Dylan and pretty soon I'll have a new baby as well. Which means Prescott has to make a lot more money than he does now. That's why we're so excited about his friend James asking him to work on the San Francisco Bay Bridge. It will pay him a much higher salary than what he makes working in Brandiss."

Rafe wrinkled his nose and kicked the leg of the table.

"If Pres works with James in the city, it will mean better pay, medical insurance, money for when he retires. All kinds of fantastic things that we all need as a family. And we're a big family, Rafe. We'll have four children in December and it costs a lot of money for all the things we need to live, to eat, and clothes for the six of us."

"What about all my new friends here?" He looked as if he was going to cry at any moment.

"I know it's sad to think of leaving your friends but think about this. If we move to Alameda, you can call your old buddies in Sausalito. They could come over to our new house, and I'll take you to visit them in Sausalito. Sausalito's maybe a thirty-minute drive from Alameda."

"We went to Alameda once for a soccer game. It's an island, right?"

She recalled their conversation about how they made Alameda into an island by dredging canals and filling them with water from the San Francisco Bay.

"Yes, and it has three bridges and an underwater tunnel. You and I drove through the tunnel to get there."

"The Posey Tube."

"The what?"

"The tunnel's called the Posey Tube. Remember?"

Annie laughed. "I'm afraid not. Your memory's much better than mine."

He looked across the table at Prescott and his mom, his face serious again. "When would we move? Soon?"

"Prescott and I think it would be best to move into our new home before the baby arrives which means we'd move at the beginning of

December. That gives you a couple of months to be with your friends." She paused. "How about we have a big going-away birthday party on October twenty-first? You could invite all your pals for a barbecue and we could have cake and ice cream like we do every year."

A bit of a smile formed on his lips, not huge, but it was better than his previous frown. "Okay."

Prescott cleared his throat. He and Annie both looked at Rafe.

"I promise this will be the last time we move," Prescott said. "Alameda will be our home for a long, long time, Rafe. This job offer from my friend is for at least seven years. You'll be in high school before the job is even finished."

"You promise?" Rafe said.

"I promise." Prescott stretched out his hand for Rafe to shake.

Rafe gave Prescott's hand a firm squeeze.

Prescott stood, still holding onto Rafe's small hand, and pulled him in for a hug. Rafe squeezed Prescott's waist, his eyes shut tight, then opened his eyes, noticed Annie watching him and smiled. And her heart felt full.

Dylan walked into the kitchen, eyes puffy from his nap. He reached out to Rafe and pulled on his sleeve. "I wanna swing."

The two boys ran out the back door and left Prescott and Annie alone.

Prescott shook his head. "Your son's pretty incredible."

Annie stared out the window into the backyard where Rafe was pushing Dylan on the swing. "We both decided to leave Sausalito but I'm the one who suggested it. He loves living here in Brandiss but his home was always in the Bay Area."

Prescott reached over and grasped her hand. "Let's make this another mission. To go where none of us has gone before. To Alameda. And I'll play Captain Kirk."

She laughed. "Does that make me Spock?"

He pushed the hair away from her face. "Your ears aren't the right shape."

She laughed, stood, and sat in his lap. "I love this old house, but I grew up in the Bay Area. It's home for me, too. We have a lot to be thankful for, Prescott."

He wrapped his arms around her waist and gave her a thorough kiss. When they came up for air, he whispered, "Then you'll be going back home."

CHAPTER THIRTY-TWO

Prescott and Annie spent the next few days searching the internet for homes in Alameda and decided to set up an appointment with a realtor.

They wanted to sell both their houses. With the money from the two sales, they'd pay cash for a new home in the Bay Area.

Abby and her friend Marge volunteered to take care of the kids while Prescott and Annie drove to Alameda. Since Prescott and Annie pre-qualified for the home loan, they had to find a house they both liked, then escrow would close shortly. If all went according to plan, they'd move into their new home the first week in December.

Prescott and Annie set off for their house-hunting tour north on 101 and arrived in Alameda in the afternoon. Their appointment with the realtor, Susan Winter, wasn't until ten the next morning and they already had reservations at the Bay Street Bed and Breakfast.

Both of them were anxious to rest after the seven hour drive. They plopped down on the oh-so-comfortable king-size bed and Prescott reached out for Annie and pulled her toward him. "You hungry?"

She rubbed her huge belly. She was almost eight months along and carried all the baby's weight in the front. "Just tired. You?"

He laid a chaste kiss on her lips and spread his hands over her belly. "I remember when Patti was pregnant with Dylan. It was always so weird when I'd feel him moving around inside. Creepy, but fun."

"Do you miss her?"

"You mean Patti?"

She nodded.

He massaged her abdomen and his hands moved up towards her ever-growing breasts to knead her nipples with his fingers. "No. But I do miss making love to you."

Her breathing escalated. Heat radiated between her legs. "You know what you do to me, Pres?"

He moaned, too involved in sucking her left breast through the cotton of her shirt.

"You drive this pregnant lady crazy." She ran her hands through his hair and gently pushed him lower. Seconds later, pulsing sensations exploded within her abdomen, lightning fast.

"Annie, Annie, Annie," he murmured and kissed his way up her neck. "Very, very pregnant and as sexy as ever."

She tried to catch her breath and felt exquisitely lethargic. "Your turn," she murmured. Her fingers slowly roved toward the top of his jeans.

He took her hands in his, brought them to his lips and kissed her fingertips. "This one's on me, Annie. You need your rest."

She gently slid her hands from his, reached under his shirt and ran her fingers through the thick hair covering his chest. He groaned her name, placed his hands over hers and tried to still their movement.

But they were never, ever alone, and Annie wasn't going to miss this opportunity to give him the pleasure he'd just given her. She pushed herself lower, eye level with the zipper of his jeans. Her fingers pulled on the tab of the zipper, and she kissed the dark hair above the rim of his jeans.

As she brought the zipper to its end, his erection pressed against her hand, stiff and wide. She knew he couldn't, and wouldn't, put up any more resistance, already past the point of no return.

He repeated her name but she was too involved in pulling down the elastic of his jockeys. His reaction was equal to hers, lightning fast, pulsing hard, and she whispered, "That one's on me."

* * * *

They woke up early the next morning. Annie hadn't slept so soundly in months. No baby crying, no bottle feeding, no alarm. They had time to shower and have a quick breakfast before they drove the short distance to Susan Winter's office.

She was an attractive woman in her mid-fifties with blonde hair, dressed impeccably in a business suit, perky bow-tie, and high heels, her attitude friendly but business-like.

The first two houses needed too much renovation with too little character. The third house, located across the street from one of the city's six parks, had two stories, a large front yard, and a back yard with a huge weeping willow tree in the middle, rose bushes in full bloom lining the fence.

The inside had been meticulously kept in its original state. The front room walls were lined with double-hung windows overlooking the yard. Built-in glass cabinets hung in the dining room, separated by a pocket door made of tiny panes of glass. The kitchen had been renovated. Dark wood stairs led to a sprawling second floor with a master bedroom and bath. Three additional bedrooms and two bathrooms were on the second floor and above it an enormous attic.

A school, located not far from the house, made it very convenient for Rafe and Dylan. This was it. They spoke with the credit union and scheduled a meeting with Susan the next day to make a formal offer on the house .

Susan suggested they drive to the Park Street area for dinner, where they found Angela's Bistro, a lovely restaurant located next to the historic Alameda Theatre. After being seated, they relaxed at a comfortable table that faced Central Avenue, with a perfect view of the cars and people passing by.

Two women strolled in front of the window with a chocolate Lab. They stopped to let a toddler pet their dog.

"What do you think, Annie?" Prescott asked.

"Rafe's been asking for a dog since he was a toddler."

He laughed out load. "I meant what do you think about the house, about Alameda?"

It was Annie's turn to laugh. "I love it. Alameda has a certain atmosphere, like home already, you know?"

He nodded. "Susan told me the population hovers around eighty thousand. There's no traffic to speak of, either. I like that."

"Me, too. I love the old Victorian houses. The city has an air of antiquity about it."

"No bad memories haunting you?" he said, a serious expression on his face.

"Nope." She shook her head. "This is nothing like Sausalito." She rubbed her protruding belly. "I could eat a horse."

He smiled. "It's an offense punishable by law to eat horse meat in California."

She leaned back and tried to get into a comfortable position. "I haven't eaten meat in years and you know it. What do you think about this place?"

"I'm happy if you're happy, Annie. All the small streets, old houses, parks. Everything's very quaint."

"It's much bigger than Brandiss, and definitely not so isolated. San Francisco's just across the Bay Bridge. You won't have far to go for work, either."

"I'll have to call James, tell him we found a house."

"It's everything we wanted, Pres. And there's nothing you need to fix."

"According to James, I won't have much free time anyway. I won't be able to join you on the couch, eating bonbons and sipping lattes all day."

They laughed, enjoying their time alone together. The meal was delicious, but Annie was anxious to head back to the B&B. They needed to call Abby to check on the kids and she was tired, having been on her feet most of the day. After their meeting with Susan the next day, they planned to head back to Brandiss.

After signing the forms and submitting their offer on the house at Susan's office the next morning, they made it back to Brandiss by dinner time, and the kids greeted them as if they'd been gone for a month. Annie felt lucky to have their little family, glad the children got along well and were happy together. It was truly a blessing.

CHAPTER THIRTY-THREE

Prescott and Annie signed the necessary documents at a sister office in Carpinteria. Escrow would close on November thirty-first. They were given the go ahead to move into their new home on the first of December.

They took a break from packing and sat on the front room couch.

Prescott took her hand, brought it to his lips and kissed her palm. "I've got good news. We can get married in January."

"A winter wedding?"

A serious expression formed on his face. "I guess a honeymoon is out of the question, huh?"

She pursed her lips. "I don't think we could pull it off. Rafe, Dylan, Jack, and a new baby? We won't know anyone in such a short time in Alameda that we could trust to take care of all the kids."

"Yeah. Three kids and a newborn would be a daunting job for any normal person."

Annie laughed out loud. "Any normal person? What does that make me?"

He reached over and pulled her closer to him. "No one ever said you were normal, Annie. You're extraordinary." He gave her a chaste kiss. "I've known James for years, but I'd never ask him and Kathleen to take care of four kids. And we've already heard Rafe's opinion about separating him from Jack."

She couldn't help grinning. "He doesn't want to be apart from him. He's very protective."

"He took it pretty hard when Allessandra changed her mind. I don't think he ever got over it."

"I think it's something he'll always feel strongly about. He has such a strong bond with Jack. He told me they're brothers now so they have to stick together forever."

She kissed him on the cheek and ran her tongue along his

jawline and down the side of his neck. He moaned and pulled her toward his chest, her breasts pressed against him.

"I really don't mind if we have to delay our honeymoon, Annie." His kisses began at her forehead, made their way slowly down her neck and stopped at the cleavage pouting over the edge of her blouse.

She was having a hard time concentrating. "Pres... we've got a ton... of... packing... to do."

He didn't pause as his hands massaged her breasts over the cotton material. "I know."

She placed her hands over his as they both squeezed her breasts. She leaned back and gazed at the ceiling, millions of zinging sensations bursting in her groin.

He stopped pinching her nipples. "Did you hear something?"

It was Jack. He'd woken from his nap. They both shook their heads and Annie chuckled.

"You find this funny?" he asked.

He was ready for way more action than a little making out on the sofa. She kissed him one last time before she got off the couch to head upstairs.

Annie turned toward him. "I guess we'd better get used to it. It'll only get worse after I have the baby. I believe they call it "intercourse interruptus"."

He tossed a pillow across the front room that hit her in the butt. She stopped and turned toward him. "If you can't stand the heat, get out of the kitchen, Pres."

He vaulted off the couch, pretended to chase her up the stairs and reached her before she made it to the top.

"I can't wait for you to be my wife," he said and grabbed her from behind.

She sat on the carpet at the top of the stairs, grasped his shirt and pulled him down. "And I can't wait for you to be my husband. You make me so happy, Pres."

Jack's tiny cries escalated to loud wails. Their alone time had come to an end. She struggled to a sitting position. "I've got to feed the baby."

Prescott shook his head. "You're not going anywhere. I'll get his bottle. You relax." He kissed her on the nose before he jogged into the nursery to get Jack.

How did she get so lucky?

* * * *

It took a week to pack their things. The movers did the majority of the hard work, wrapped up the larger items, covered the furniture with moving blankets, put everything in the moving van. Susan planned to drop the house keys in the mailbox on the day of their arrival and the movers would arrive the day after. Everything was flowing according to schedule.

They drove separate cars from Brandiss. Prescott took Dylan with him in the truck, and Rafe and Jack stayed with Annie. When they drove over the Park Street Bridge into Alameda, Annie let out a sigh of relief. Driving for seven hours had taken its toll.

Her due date was fast approaching, and she felt uncomfortable sitting for long periods of time. They pulled up to 1716 Lauren Drive and parked in the driveway. They ended one journey and were beginning a new one.

Prescott hurried over to help her out of the car. Her huge belly made it difficult to maneuver around the steering wheel.

He tried not to laugh but the inklings of a smile appeared on his lips.

"What's so funny?" She struggled to stand.

"I'll just call you Grace." She gave him a quizzical look. "You know, as in graceful."

Annie gave him a dirty look. "Will you just give me a hand here? I swear this kid is going to weigh thirteen pounds!"

He grabbed the diaper bag and swung it over his shoulder. He grasped her hands and helped her stand.

He chuckled under his breath. "Do you want to make a bet on how much the kid weighs? Twenty bucks says he weighs nine pounds, six ounces."

Her eyes widened. "Did you say he?" She let out a derisive laugh. "I think not."

Rafe helped Dylan out of the truck and Prescott leaned over to unfasten Jack's car seat.

"We don't have time to argue now, Annie. But the baby's a boy. I can feel it." He glanced at Rafe. "What do you think? Boy or girl?"

Rafe shrugged. "I don't have any money."

"See?" she said. "All bets are off." She took Dylan's hand, and looked at Rafe. "This Monday I register you and Dylan at Paden Elementary School. Prescott starts his new job that day, too. We have a lot of things to look forward to."

Together they walked to the front door, Jack perched on top of her protruding stomach. Prescott turned the key and opened the big wooden door. Rafe and Dylan ran inside the house, their footsteps on the hardwood floors echoed off the walls.

"Where's my bedroom?" Rafe shouted and raced up the stairs with Dylan behind him, taking each stair one at a time.

"You two can fight over who gets which room later, guys," Prescott shouted up at them. "We've got to get our stuff out of the truck." He turned toward Annie, where she stood blocking the doorway. "Wait!" He put up his index finger. "Should I try carrying you over the threshold?"

She gave him a look of mock disgust and placed Jack in his arms. "My back's killing me." She leaned against the door jamb. "And you're not funny, Pres. I can't wait for tomorrow when the movers arrive so I can lie on the couch."

He smiled. "Shall I bring in your box of bonbons?"

"Again, not funny, Pres. I need my sleeping bag. Could you get it out of the truck for me?" She waddled into the front room and plopped down none too gracefully on the hardwood floor.

They spent the night "camping" in the front room, sleeping bags strewn over the floor. The next day the movers arrived and by Sunday night everything was in place.

Monday arrived quicker than she thought possible. Prescott was already on the road by six a.m., and she took Rafe and Dylan to Paden School at eight o'clock to complete their registrations. She didn't have to pick them up until three p.m.

Annie couldn't wait to return home to be alone with Jack. It would be the start of a new routine for her in Alameda. The sound of silence that morning when she put him down for his nap was music to her ears. She laid down on the couch in the front room, listened to the sweet trills of the birds in the trees and the branches blowing in the fall breeze. How perfect her life was.

By mid-week, Rafe and Dylan were enjoying their new school, teachers and classmates. Prescott spent a lot of time with James Dunsmuir on the Bay Bridge project.

Annie was reading e-mails on her MacBook when she felt the first sharp pain in her lower back. She knew what it meant. She could have used a few more days to get accustomed to their new life in Alameda, but now that wasn't going to happen.

CHAPTER THIRTY-FOUR

Annie called Prescott on his cell but when he answered, loud clanging of machinery thrummed in the background.

"Hello?" he yelled.

"I'm going into labor." The noise was so loud, she wasn't sure whether he could hear.

"I'll meet you at the hospital within the hour," he shouted. "I'll call Kathleen. She'll drive you to the hospital. She'll take care of the kids. Just like we planned. Okay?"

The pain was getting worse and she found it hard to concentrate. "Okay." She made it over to the couch and lay down as another pain stabbed her in the back. She took deep breaths, tried to relax and exhaled slowly.

She hadn't had the opportunity to meet her new obstetrician, Dr. Lillian Frank. Her doctor in Sea Cliff had already sent her file, and when Annie phoned the office, the nurse said Dr. Frank would meet Annie at the hospital.

James's wife, Kathleen, drove up to the house within minutes. Prescott had already given her a key and she let herself in.

"Annie? It's Kathleen," she called out. She came around the corner with a worried expression. "Are you alright? Is the pain bad?"

Annie closed her eyes and tried to concentrate on her personal picture—the ocean with waves crashing on the beach, a full moon setting over the horizon.

"I'm doing fine, believe it or not. You probably know what it's like." Immediately after saying the words, a niggling bit of information in the back of Annie's mind told her she'd committed the ultimate faux pas.

Kathleen smiled and shook her head. "I haven't had the pleasure. James and I tried in vitro three times. We're giving it a rest for now."

Annie tried to sit up and another wave of pain shot through her lower back. She grimaced and fell back onto the cushions. Kathleen knelt down beside the couch.

"I'm... so... sorry," Annie said between gasps for air. "Prescott told me about your experience but I forgot."

Kathleen took hold of Annie's hand. "Don't think anything of it. This isn't the time to be discussing me. Right now we have to get you to the hospital."

Kathleen helped her off the couch and guided Annie to the car parked in the driveway. Kathleen returned to get Jack out of his crib, buckled him in the car seat, and drove to the hospital. Annie leaned against the car door as waves of contractions gripped her abdomen every few minutes.

If memory served her right, everything was proceeding on schedule. It brought back memories of when she'd gone into labor with Rafe. Cameron drove like Mario Andretti on their way to the hospital in San Francisco back then.

When Kathleen pulled up to the emergency room, several members of the staff greeted them and helped settle Annie in a wheel chair.

Kathleen leaned over and kissed her on the cheek. "I've gotta go, Annie. I'll take Jack back to your house and pick up Rafe and Dylan at school later."

It took longer than Annie expected to fill out the appropriate forms. Afterward, one of the staff wheeled her to the Birthing Room, took her vital signs, and helped her undress. The nurse was assisting her into bed when Annie heard Prescott's voice. He entered the room like a wind storm had blown him through the door. He sat on the edge of the bed and leaned over to give her a quick kiss.

"How're you doing, babe?" he said, his face pale.

She knew he was worried. He'd never told her about Dylan's birth or whether he'd been Patti's birthing coach, so Annie wasn't sure how new this experience was for him.

She started to answer him, when another, much stronger contraction tore into her lower back, like a jagged saber, the pain excruciating.

Prescott stood next to the bed and held her hand. He looked as if he would faint or vomit. At some point, Annie must have passed out.

When she opened her eyes, an oxygen mask covered her nose and mouth.

She pulled the mask away. "How long have I been out?"

"Just a few seconds," he said. "All I can say is I wouldn't switch places with you for a million bucks."

"I couldn't catch my breath."

He nodded and wiped the sweat from her face with a wet cloth. "Dr. Frank said it shouldn't be much longer."

She grimaced as another contraction ripped through her belly.

"Breathe deeply, Annie," he urged.

Annie suddenly felt the need to push at the same time as Dr. Frank said, "Annie, I think it's time. Bear down as hard as you can."

She held onto the sides of the bed rails and pushed so hard through the pain she heard her own scream as if coming from someone else. Her head pounded, her heart beat as though it would pop out of her chest.

"Once more will do it, Annie. Push as hard as you can," the doctor called out.

Annie pushed again. Her forehead almost touched the top of her huge belly. She felt the head coming out, and then the sudden rush of what she knew was the body and legs of her baby.

"It's a girl!" Dr. Frank smiled at Annie with her eyes above the mask that covered the bottom half of her face.

Prescott placed his arm around Annie's back for support so she could watch Dr. Frank lift up their daughter. The doctor turned the baby in their direction to give them a quick glimpse, and then passed the tiny newborn to the nurse to aspirate the fluid from the baby's throat.

While the doctor massaged Annie's abdomen to remove the afterbirth, an enormous wave of peacefulness flowed through her.

"We have a daughter," Annie whispered.

"Would you like to hold your baby?" the doctor asked, holding their little girl, wrapped in a white blanket.

Annie nodded, her throat clogged with emotion. Hugging the baby to her chest, she glanced over at Prescott, his eyes glistened with unshed tears. "Christine, meet your daddy."

They watched the nurses wash Christine, measure her, and perform the Apgar test. It was such a relief to be free of the pain,

Annie felt energized and awake. Prescott sat on the side of the bed, holding a squirming little bundle in his arms.

He placed Christine on Annie's stomach, and she gently wrapped her arms around the baby. Annie pulled back the top edge of the blanket to reveal their daughter's tiny pink face.

"She's beautiful," Annie said and glanced up at Prescott. "And she's healthy."

"She's perfect." His smile widened. "All ten toes, ten fingers, strong lungs. And she scored high on the Apgar, too."

Annie couldn't pull her eyes away from her child. Christine had a lovely round head with a crown of dark brown hair and skin so pink and soft, Annie couldn't stop brushing her face along Christine's tiny forehead while holding the baby's itsy-bitsy hand in her thumb and forefinger.

"Ten pounds, one ounce," he said, shaking his head.

"I know." Annie laughed. "No wonder I felt like I was going to pop."

"She probably won't even fit in the newborn clothes we bought." He paused. "When can you nurse her?"

"Right now. I nursed Rafe when he was only a few hours old."

Annie pulled aside the hospital gown to reveal her breast. Christine's heart-shaped lips nuzzled the nipple, latching on immediately, her little fist pressed against Annie's chest. Droplets of breast milk clung to her bright-red tongue as she began to suckle. Barely audible swallowing noises escaped from her throat.

Prescott kissed the top of Annie's head.

"That's the most beautiful picture I've ever seen. You feeding our daughter for the first time." Several tears coursed their way through the stubble on his cheeks.

"It's like falling in love for the first time," she said.

He sat on the side of the bed and leaned in toward Annie. "I am the luckiest man on the planet. I love you so much." He took Christine's hand in his fingers and bent down to give her a soft kiss on the cheek. "She's almost as beautiful as you, Annie. She'll knock 'em dead when she's a teenager."

Annie loved the fact she was sharing these precious first moments with Prescott and knew she'd remember them for the rest of her life. She fell asleep soon afterward and awoke to the dim light shining through the hospital shades and the clink of breakfast trays and low words of greeting amongst the patients and staff. She opened her eyes to find Prescott asleep in the chair next to the bed, lightly snoring.

As soon as the doctor checked Annie and Christine, they were released. Prescott helped Annie get dressed, she signed the necessary release papers, and the nurse wheeled her down to the front door of the hospital where Prescott brought his truck into the curved driveway and helped her into the front seat.

Within a few minutes they arrived home. Rafe and Dylan were in school and Jack was spending the day with Kathleen. Prescott and Annie were both anxious to have them all here to meet their new baby sister.

When he picked the boys up from school, he stopped by to get Jack at the Dunsmuir's house. The two boys ran into the house and came to a screeching halt when they saw Annie sitting on the couch, Christine asleep in her arms.

Annie looked up at Rafe and Dylan, a wave of pure sweetness filled her heart. "This is Christine, your baby sister."

Their family was complete.

CHAPTER THIRTY-FIVE

January arrived sunny and cool, the temperature around sixty degrees, no clouds in a light blue sky. A bit of a breeze lightly tossed the tips of the leaves on the trees in the back yard. Standing beneath them seemed almost surreal, like something out of a fairy tale.

Their guests began arriving at four o'clock. They served vegetable lasagna, roasted chicken, rice pilaf, fresh steamed vegetables, and French bread. The white wedding cake had been decorated with three tiers. A hand-carved chocolate bride and groom stood in the middle of each tier.

The chairs, decorated with white lace and tiny yellow roses, stood on the neatly trimmed lawn in front of a small raised dais where the wedding ceremony would be performed. The Justice of the Peace had arrived and was ready to begin.

They hired a young musician from the university, a harpist, who began playing a soulful rendition of the wedding march. Annie walked up the short aisle to meet with Prescott, lips trembling, legs shaky.

They turned toward each other, clasped their hands together and vowed to love and trust one another within the bond of matrimony.

"I present to you Prescott and Annie Beemiller," the Justice of the Peace announced in a hardy voice. "The groom may now kiss the bride to seal their everlasting commitment to each other."

Prescott lifted her veil and they kissed, caught up in the moment that marked the beginning of their life together as husband and wife. Seconds passed before their friends clapped and they broke apart. They laughed, held hands, and walked back down the aisle to greet their guests.

After dinner was served, Prescott and Annie visited each table and talked to people they hadn't seen in months or even years.

The sun set and the children slowed down. Everyone pitched in to take care of Rafe, Jack, Dylan, and Christine to allow Prescott and Annie extra time to enjoy themselves.

As solar powered lights along the paths turned on, the celebration wound down and the caterers cleaned up. Prescott and Annie were anxious to have some time alone. Abby and her friends had put the children to bed and Christine had been asleep for hours in the nursery. Prescott and Annie were grateful for their help.

Abby waved goodbye and quietly shut the front door. The silence of the night descended, and the newlyweds retired to their favorite couch in the front room.

Exhausted, they smiled at each other. Their lives together were just beginning and it was so much different than Annie would have imagined.

Prescott took her in his arms and reached around to unzip her wedding gown. The bodice fell forward and revealed her braless chest and his eyes opened wide. He laughed in a low growl while he stripped the gown down her thighs to the floor.

Annie leaned back and enjoyed his attentive hands, aware of his rapidly escalating breaths. Her nipples protruded easily for his mouth, while he licked and suckled.

She was on the edge, about to scream with wanting him. He brought his face to her and her tongue searched his mouth. She ripped down the zipper of his trousers and gently pulled out his engorged shaft. He gasped as she stroked him firmly. He hovered over her, his erection hard and full, reached for the tips of her breasts and grazed her nipples. He moved slowly downward, found that perfect place he was meant to be, and slipped easily inside.

Annie bent her head back, lost in the waves of her orgasm. Prescott whispered her name, riding his own crest of ecstasy.

He carried her up the long flight of stairs to their bedroom and they fell asleep to the sound of the night doves outside the window.

The day was ending and their happily ever after had just begun.

THE END

About the Author

Born and raised in the San Francisco Bay Area, Patricia attended St. Mary's College, studied her junior year at the University of Madrid, received a B.A. in Spanish at UC Santa Barbara then went on to get a Master's degree in Education at Oregon State University. She lives with her husband and two children in Alameda, across the bay from San Francisco, along with three chocolate labs, Jack, UJE, and Remy. Her Friesian horse Maximus lives in the Oakland hills in a stall with a million dollar view.